SUPERN...
Dating...

Here for
the
Seer

ANDIE M. LONG

CHAPTER 1

EBONY

Friday 9 February 2018

I'd always seen my visions as a curse... until I'd lost them.

Last week I'd been in my clothing boutique in Withernsea as usual, unpacking new stock, and then the next minute everything had gone blank. My heart had lurched when I'd realised my visions were gone and I'd dashed out of the shop, crashing into Jax's coffee shop next door. I thought the lack of visions meant my death was imminent, but thankfully, my friend Frankie had assured me that was a myth.

After a few days of resting at my friend Shelly's house where I'd felt like I was on holiday, I started to miss them. My thoughts were the company I had when alone, the glimpse into the exciting times ahead for people, the feeling of usefulness when I could warn of danger. Without them I was... redundant.

Finally, it transpired that my vodka had been tampered with (a few voddies helped with the thoughts when they became too much, and helped prevent migraines), and I'd been informed my visions would return fully within two weeks.

It had been such a relief to discover the blame lay with an errant warlock who had been trying to prevent me warning my friends about the wicked plans of a rogue werewolf. Luckily, he'd been thwarted and now while I waited for my visions to return, I was going to witness one of my predictions coming true. My friend Kim was marrying a werewolf called Darius. God, it had taken a while for it to sink into the stubborn woman's head...

Of course, my visions would decide to return during the wedding reception. I guess it could have been worse, but one minute I was dancing to 'Celebration' and the next the pain hit. I dragged myself over to the nearest empty seat and clutching the nearby table top, I lowered myself onto the chair.

"Someone's had a bit too much champagne," I heard one of the new wolves of the Withernsea pack say.

"No. That's Ebony," the other replied. "Watch her eyes and face. It's creepy as fuck."

I knew what they'd be watching. My eyes would roll until the whites were exposed and my face would take on a grey pallor. I'd heard all the insults many times before: creepy, crazy, alcoholic.

The black haze came over and the vision played in my mind like I was watching on a cinema screen.

I let it play out and then I screamed.

Vision over, I opened my eyes to see that the new big burly werewolf was holding onto the other pack member for dear life. Idiot. But I had bigger problems. I ran outside to find Kim.

Running through the edge of the woods, I entered the canopy of trees and ran into the centre where I spotted her with her new husband Darius. Thank God they weren't in the middle of sex because this couldn't wait.

"They're back. Kim, the voices are back," I yelled.

I caught the bitch's eye roll as she told me I hadn't needed to rush back to tell her that. No, 'Thanks so much for my handsome new husband, how can I now help you?' She was too busy thinking of his dick, and no that hadn't come to me in a vision, she was looking at his crotch like a dog sat by a Sunday roast.

"But you were in my vision..." I needed her help this time around.

Darius looked worried, not surprising since his sister had recently had to kill two rogue werewolves. "What did you see, Ebony?"

"I saw a wedding dress. I was wearing it, and I was standing in a church. Kim was my bridesmaid."

Darius' expression was a mix of relief and confusion.

"I thought you weren't supposed to see your own future?" Kim queried.

"That's just it, Kim. I could see I was getting married, but I couldn't see the groom! I don't even have a boyfriend, so who the hell am I marrying?" I screamed again. It seemed I was having a bit of a panic attack when it came to my own future. Upcoming horror visions gave me migraines, my own wedding made me hysterical. I needed a little perspective, and more alcohol.

"Well, I don't know, but I do know who I just married, Chica, so you go get a vodka and I'll go get my man." Kim winked. "We'll sort it, Ebs."

And with that she abandoned me in the middle of the woodland. If I had a future vision showing she was going to give birth to eleven-pound twins I would delight in telling her in great detail.

I walked back towards the hall where the party was taking place and took a seat on the steps outside while I tried to recollect my vision. But it was fading. With other people's visions I could recall every detail, but my own was disappearing like a dream does when you awaken. Maybe it was because my visions were only just returning, or maybe it was because they were mine.

Then slam, another pain shot into my forehead like a brain freeze.

Shelley was having the baby! I had to go back to the farm.

I ran to the bar where I ordered a double vodka to ease the throbbing in my temples. Then I ordered a taxi.

"Goodacres Farm please, and can you step on it? It's an emergency."

And it was, but not for the reasons a normal person might think...

CHAPTER 2

Y ou know how they say God doesn't give you more than you can handle in life?

Well, fuck that, and if anyone says it to my face, then 'do no harm' rules or not, I'll throat punch them and magic their mouth shut. Just when I'd thought things couldn't get any worse, my pregnancy got accelerated during my turning into a vampire, and then a couple of days later I'd gone into labour at my best friend's wedding.

One minute I was moaning about having to wear the equivalent of a marquee—I mean my dress looked big enough to hold the wedding reception underneath it, glamorous I was not—the next, my best friend ran in front of us in wolf mode having become a were and then she forgot herself and changed back, appearing starkers in front of everyone. It was hilarious. Well, until I thought I'd peed myself and then she got the last laugh by pointing out my waters had broken.

Then do you know what she did?

She left me to go boink her new husband.

Yes, her mother-in-law came to help, and yes, my own husband was there, but what sort of bestie did that? Then again, her husband had also had a period of nakedness until someone passed him a robe and, let's just say I could see why she was distracted. Plus, she'd just escaped having to marry a madman.

Still. I was having a baby...

"Oh my god, I'm having a baby."

"Not now!" yelled Theo. "It's not coming now, is it? Only I'm waiting for the taxi to come to take us home."

I'd decided on a home birth. I had a midwife at the Caves where I'd been turned who would come to make sure everything went to plan.

"Theo," I shouted at my husband who was running around the wedding reception like some kind of demented rooster, his head darting about as he questioned other guests. I watched as he collected unused napkins from every table.

"Theo!" I yelled louder, even though I knew with his vampire hearing he could hear me anyway.

He ran over.

"What are you doing?"

He pushed his dark hair back off his face. "They say towels and hot water don't they? There aren't any towels but there are napkins. I can grab a bottle of Evian too."

Staring at him I rolled my eyes. "I'm not giving birth to a frikkin Barbie doll. There's a large melon coming out. The napkins will only be any use for you to wipe your sweating brow on if you don't get a grip. Now, Theo. What is wrong with the fact you have ordered a taxi?"

He paused for a moment. "Erm, early hours of Saturday

morning it costs double and there are a lack of available cabs?"

I went to grab my temple in frustration from his idiocy, but a contraction chose that moment to decide to sweep over me.

"Holy fucking Christ." I took some deep breaths.

For crying out loud. I'd only had my last period pains a couple of months ago, then the pain of the turning this week, and now I was having these agonising labour pains.

I felt a hand stroking down my arm. "Breathe, darling. It's okay. Just a little pain."

God, I would put laxatives in his O-neg when I'd had this child.

"Theo, I'll see you at home. You take the cab if you want. Idiot." I whizzed off. How do you forget you can travel at high speed? That was the first indication of the escalating panic levels of one Theodore Robert Landry.

"You all right, lovey?" My mother-in-law followed me into the living room.

"I'm in labour, Mary. Just need to phone Janice at the clinic and get her here."

"I'll do that for you. You get laid down on the sofa. Oooh, how exciting, my first grandchild is coming." Mary went to pick up the phone and her hand passed through it. "Ooops, I think I expended too much energy watching *Magic Mike* this afternoon on DVD. I was trying to perfect that 'Pony' dance like his soon-to-be-ex-wife did. You know, just in case Channing's looking for a new woman."

Mary was a ghost, having been drained by Theo when he was first turned. It was a subject we tried not to dwell on. We therefore had a ghost perpetually in her late-thirties living with us and she'd just begun realising the freedoms that came from not living in the early 1900's.

"Go rest, Mary, because I will need you later."

"To care for the baby? I'm great with them. I was a natural with Theo you know? One reason my ghost heart was heavy when I realised he'd killed me."

Theo whizzed in at that moment, banging his head on the door frame, then laying sprawled across the living room floor. "Yes, to care for the baby," I replied. "The one right there." I kicked him with my shoe, and he groaned so I figured he was still conscious.

Picking up my mobile phone I called the clinic, and once I knew Janice was on her way, I sat back, resting on the sofa for a while and breathing through a few contractions. Theo sat at the side of me and as I noted the look of worry on his face, my mood just calmed. The guy loved me, he loved our baby, and he wanted us to be safe and well.

I took his hand in mine. "I love you, Theo Landry."

"I love you too, Mrs Theo Landry."

"What have I told you about that old-fashioned crap?"

"I'm 127. Bite me."

That made me giggle. Looked like I was teaching Theo a thing or two about sass.

"Sorry, I've been moody. I'm just a little scared. I've not had a baby before."

"Don't worry, I'm used to your moods." He patted my arm. "And this is about my hundredth baby."

I shot back away from him. "What the what now?"

"This." He pointed at my stomach. "I think." He nodded his head. "Yes, I'm almost positive this is about the hundredth birth."

My jaw went tight. "You. Have. Had. One. Hundred. Children?"

"Well, not me personally. The mother's obviously. You do crack me up."

"And where are all these offspring?" I was going to drain the bastard in a minute. Not once had he mentioned previously having children.

"Offspring?" Theo's brow creased. "They're not my offspring. They are the babies I delivered while I was an obstetrician in the 1960's."

I took a deep breath.

"Of course medicine was a lot different then, but still I shall offer my expertise to Janice."

As my next contraction hit, I used my vampire strength to its full capacity to crush his fingers hard. "Or maybe you could just be quiet and let me get on with the childbirth, my loving husband?"

"Ow-ow-ow-ow-ow." He extracted his fingers as I let go. "I thought you were sorry for being mean?"

Tilting my head, I smiled at him, possibly reminiscent of the Joker in Batman. "I'm trying, but it's the hormones."

The doorbell rang. "Ah, I shall go get that. It will be the midwife." He rushed off, still stretching out his recently crushed fingers.

Janice poked her head around the door. She was a small woman with a dark-brown bob, and she wore glasses. "How are you doing there?"

Theo walked past her and sat back down beside me on

the sofa. "Well, my head is hurting from hitting the door frame earlier, and my fingers are hurting from where Shelley crushed them, but other than that, I'm doing okay."

"She meant me, douche canoe," I yelled as yet another contraction hit.

Janice smiled at me with a bemused look. "Gotta love the husbands. Now, don't worry, Theo, we're a team and we're going to get that baby out safely. How far apart are the contractions, Shelley?"

"Every three minutes."

"Right, let's get you upstairs onto the bed and get everything prepared. You doing this without pain relief?"

"Well, that was the plan, but I might yet throw him out." I glared at my husband.

"She's going to use magic just before the birth to assist our daughter on her way. Her mother helped her to construct a spell."

"Oh yes, we have that on the birth plan. Okay, Theo, why don't you get your wife a glass of water? I'll take a tea, and then you get whatever you need."

"Common sense," I mumbled under my breath.

"I can hear you," Theo said. "Excuse me, Janice. Could I have a little word with you outside?"

She looked at me, cocking an eyebrow, and then turned to Theo. "Sure, sweetheart. Only a minute though, I need to concentrate on your wife. Shelley, can you change into this gown for me while we're gone?"

"Sure," I said as she followed him outside.

Theo took care to make sure I couldn't hear despite my vampire hearing. It was a shame for him that he appeared to have forgotten I was part-witch. I made a hand swipe motion and a vision of Theo talking to the midwife appeared in front of me.

"Could you please phone an exorcist? I have the means to pay for one to travel here expeditiously."

Janice leaned in closer to him. "You've lost me, Theo. Why do we need an exorcist?"

He gestured to the room. "Well, clearly, Shelley has been possessed. We were out at a wedding when she went into labour. I didn't know all of the guests. One of them must have been an evil entity as Shelley has most definitely been taken over by something malevolent. I was an obstetrician for a while and never did I come across such evil."

"Your wife is acting perfectly normal for someone in childbirth."

His eyes widened. "She is?"

"Yes, so shall we get back up to her before she begins to give birth without us and then you'll really know what evil looks like." She placed a hand on his arm. "Stay calm, focus on your wife and baby, and soon this will all be over, and you'll have your baby girl."

"And then my wife will be back to her nicer self?"

"With sleep deprivation and sore nipples?" Janice cackled with laughter. "Oh, Theo. You've a lot to learn for someone so old."

I wiped the vision away and quickly changed into my gown before stroking at my stomach. "Hey there, baby girl. Not long now and you're gonna be here."

Then an almighty wave of pain spliced across my stomach. I felt like I was being sliced in two. My breath came in short gasps, and I knew there wasn't much further to go. As the pain receded, I said a few magic enchantments. A haze came over the bottom half of my body and when the next pain came, it was considerably lessened.

I laid back, pulled my knees up and pushed.

"She's crowning." Janice rushed back to my side. "Theo. Business end."

I closed my eyes and pushed once more.

"Waaaaaahhhhhhhhhh."

My daughter was checked quickly and then placed into my arms.

"Theo, will you get that little baby hat from the top drawer? I don't want her to lose any heat from her head."

Theo brought the cute little hat over and placed it on our daughter's head. He reached down and kissed my forehead and then ran a finger over our baby girl's cheek.

"Well done, Mummy," Janice said. "And congratulations, Daddy. All normal checks have been carried out. Obviously, given her heritage, it's hard to know what to expect from her in the future, but she seems just fine."

Then our daughter opened her eyes. "Oh look, Theo. She has the normal blue eyes that a human baby has.

"Hello, Charlene. I'm your mummy and this is your daddy."

Charlene blinked. Her eyes went red and then she blinked again, and green reptilian eyes stared at me. "Jesus," I squealed.

Thank God for vampire speed, otherwise my newborn daughter would have been on the floor.

"I thought you had to be given your sea powers?" Theo frowned. "Your dad passed yours onto you."

I swear to God our daughter gave a little smile.

"That looks like a smile, but it's actually wind," Janice said. I wasn't convinced.

"Theo, I've got a feeling our daughter will be very unique." I stared at her. "Right, baby?"

CHAPTER 3

EBONY

An hour-and-a-half had passed since I'd known Shelley was in labour. Unfortunately, my own supernatural powers were limited to the visions. The vampires could whizz, the werewolves could run at speed, demons could open and travel through portals, and angels could fly. It wasn't entirely fair that I helped the universe and still had to pay for taxis, but such was my lot.

I rang the doorbell at the farmhouse and Mary answered.

To say we'd spent a large portion of the last week or so together she appeared to groan before smiling at me. "Ebony, lovely. I thought you were okay enough to stay back at your own house? Only it's a little hectic here."

"I saw the baby coming in a vision. I have to be here."

Mary bustled with pride. "She's absolutely gorgeous. Well, she looks a little weird when her eyes change, but other than that, she's just perfect."

"Erm, okay. Am I all right to go see her?"

"I'll just check. Come through to the kitchen while you wait."

Mary disappeared. She was another supernatural able to come and go, although Mary wasn't able to venture too far from where she'd been brutally slain, so there was that.

She appeared again, making me jump.

"Yes, you can go visit. Like I said, watch for the eyes. It's making everyone startle. I hope the child bounces because someone's going to freak out and drop her before long."

Slowly, I made my way up the stairs bracing myself. I expected that the minute I walked through the door I'd be hit with visions connected with the baby's future. She was going to be the most powerful ruler of Withernsea after all.

The door to the bedroom was ajar, and I could make out someone walking around and the sound of murmuring. I tapped on the door and Theo opened it wider, a massive smile on his face.

"Welcome, Ebony. Our first proper visitor! Come in and meet Charlene."

Not a single vision hit me. Perplexed, I made my way over to Shelley who was sitting in an armchair with the baby in her arms. "Look, Charlie, it's Ebony. She's come to visit you because you are so very special."

I took in the sight of the baby. She had a small amount of dark, soft downy hair on her head, and the cutest button nose. Her rosebud lips and heart-shaped face cemented the fact she was going to be a beauty. She opened her eyes and I swear to God she stared at me knowingly. It was the strangest feeling. An intense feeling of calm washed over me.

"Hello, Charlene. You are very beautiful. I'm Ebony,

and my role here is to make sure you live a safe and happy life. The thing is, I have visions, so I will always let you and your mummy know if there's any danger around." My gaze met Shelley's.

"That's why I'm here. I know it's usually close family who come first, but my visions have returned, and I need to be here as you receive visitors. The heads of all species will come to see you because of the importance of your daughter."

"I'm going to need you to get me a new make-up palette. I can't be seeing people in this state." Shelley pushed back her hair.

"You're a new mother, you look radiant and beautiful." It was a total lie. Shelley looked like she'd been dragged through a hedge backwards while a tornado happened, but you didn't tell a new mother that. She did have that new mother glow though that came with the birth endorphins. I'd get a hairbrush later and help her look a little more presentable.

"You really think Charlie could be in danger?" Shelley bit her bottom lip.

"I don't know at this point. The visions haven't revealed anything to me yet, but it's best to be cautious." I glanced at my watch. It was almost four am.

"Is it okay if I take my room again? I'll leave you to rest now."

A woman came into the room and Shelley introduced her as the midwife.

"I'm staying for the next few hours, just to make sure everything's okay and to give the new mum a chance to rest, and then if everything stays fine, I'll leave around midday? I'm sure by then all the family will have gathered around.

"Hopefully I'll be able to hold my grandbaby soon." Mary appeared in the room, a frown on her face. "Only all this caring for visitors is draining my energy, meaning other people get cuddles and I haven't had one yet."

"I haven't held the baby," I said to Mary, feeling I'd not earned the irritated look cast my way.

"Would you like to?" Shelley said. "You'll have to excuse my manners, I'm tired."

"Yes, please."

I took the baby from Shelley, ignoring Mary's thunderous expression and her large "Harrumph," before she disappeared again. That newborn smell wafted beneath my nose and for the first time ever, I wondered if I would have any children of my own.

Again, the baby's eyes opened and stared at me. It was if the baby was letting me know I would be fine. But that was impossible, surely? She was just a baby.

Not any old baby. The words appeared as clear as day in my mind.

My eyes widened, my arms wobbled, and I saw Shelley notice. "She do the eye thing again?"

"Yes," I lied. "It's quite something isn't it?"

Can you speak in my mind? I suggested to the baby, feeling rather foolish.

You betcha, but shhh, right? It's a secret. Until my body catches up with my mind.

Then a vision came. It didn't hurt. Didn't feel like my head would explode. It just floated through. A vision of Charlene.

Not a word, remember? She said through the mind bond.

Okay. I'm here to protect you though, so if I need to tell them, I will. I thought back.

Agreed.

Oh boy. Shelley and Theo were headed for one big shock.

CHAPTER 4

SHELLEY

They were telling me to rest, but I was wired. I'd just had a baby! My eyes looked at the sleeping bundle in the crib at the side of me. I felt like my heart was going to burst out of my chest. Such love, such pride, and when I watched Theo pick her up so very carefully and stare at her in awe, I wanted to bawl my eyes out with the perfectness of it all.

But a cloud overshadowed everything.

It wasn't fair.

Ebony had to be here because someone might wish my newborn baby harm. All because Charlie's future role would be to keep peace in Withernsea. Peace between land and sea, human and supernatural, species to species. For that reason, I couldn't just be a normal mother showing my baby off, thinking about our taking her on her first day of school; the girly shopping trips we'd do together where we bought far too many clothes. What would any of that be like? Would we have to have bodyguards for her?

There was a knock. I looked up and saw Theo knocking

on fresh air. He should be asleep by now. He should have been asleep since dawn, and he was struggling.

Then I realised I'd put a force field up around me and Charlie. *Oops.*

"Janice has left. She'll be back tomorrow to check on you and the baby, but she says just call her if you need her for anything. Your parents are downstairs. Are you okay to see them?" He yawned.

"I am. Theo, go get in bed now."

"Yes, I think that would be wise. If I have a few hours now, then you can sleep later while I take care of Charlene. Only it would be nice to spend a little more cuddle time with my daughter." He smiled.

"I know I'm hogging her. But I can't help myself, Theo. She's perfect." We both looked back at the crib where Charlie was still sound asleep. I didn't know how her sleeping patterns would be with her being a mix of witch, wyvern, and vampire, but so far she'd napped on and off after feeding like most babies did. She was being breastfed. Janice had said my body would give her the right mix of what she needed, both blood and milk, so I was making sure I drank and ate regularly.

Theo left and my parents came into the room.

"Oh my goodness, Shelley. What a beautiful angel you have." My mum's eyes filled with tears as she looked in the crib. My father walked over to me and hugged me, kissing my cheek. Then he also went over to the crib.

"She looks like you did as a baby, Shelley." My mum broke down then and my dad clutched her. I gave them some time to process the situation. My mum had had to give me up for adoption and my father had been tricked into Hell, so he'd only ever seen photos of me as a baby, and only in the last year once he'd been freed. For them this was a bittersweet moment.

My mum moved to hug and kiss me and then they both took seats next to my bed.

"How are you feeling, darling? Theo said the birth was quite quick?"

"Yes, just a couple of hours, so I feel very fortunate in that respect. The spell helped considerably, Mum. The first pains I experienced were incredible. I thought I was going to die. Then I did the spell and had one intense pain and then everything numbed. From then on, she couldn't wait to be born."

"That's because she knows she's going to be the most spoiled child in the universe," my dad said. "It's a good job you live in a large farmhouse with what your mum's been buying."

"Mum!"

"Well, everything happened so fast. One minute you're in your first trimester, the next the baby's coming. I went shopping before we came here and just made sure you have enough of everything you need."

"There's enough for everyone in Withernsea." My dad winked and my mum pushed him on the arm.

"Behave yourself, Dylan."

"Now where would the fun be in that?" He winked at her again.

Mum went out into the hallway and dragged in several large shopping bags and then she proceeded to unveil every possible thing a baby could need. I wouldn't need to shop again for months.

"Thanks, Mum." I laughed.

"So, we have to ask, darling." Mum's tone softened. "The name. Charlene. How did you choose it? Is it a relative of Theo's you named her after?"

I snorted. "Not quite. Theo has an unhealthy obsession with Scott and Charlene from *Neighbours*. He wouldn't hear of her being called anything else. Luckily for him, I liked it."

"Theo is so lucky." My dad started to sing Kylie's hit and me and my mum both groaned.

"Look at that. Charlene is smiling. She thinks Grandad's funny, don't you, Charlene?"

"It's just wind, Dad."

My mum's face went wistful again. "I wish we'd been able to keep you, to stay together. That you could have experienced our love for you. I know you had a rough deal from your adoptive parents. Are they coming by the way?"

"Yes, on Monday, and they're bringing Polly." Polly was their younger daughter, my kind-of sister in that we'd been brought up together, though she'd been given a lot more attention than I had. My adoptive parents and I had a strained relationship, but had recently made more of an effort to try to get along once I'd realised a lot of what had happened had been borne from fear about my supernatural abilities.

"They weren't all bad. I had some fun times with them too. Just not very often," I told them. "But I got by and turned out okay."

"You turned out more than okay. We are beyond proud of the young woman and new mother you have become," my father said. "We wish we could have been responsible for your childhood, but then you wouldn't necessarily have met Theo and had this beautiful little baby, so things must have been meant to be that way."

Charlene stirred in her cot and then opened her eyes. "Do you want to get her, Mum?"

My mum picked her up and sat back in the chair with her. She rocked her slightly while she spoke to her softly. "I'm your grandma and I love you so very much. I'm going nowhere, Charlene. Me and your grandad will be here when we can. We will make some beautiful memories." Then she seemed to become lost in her thoughts. A minute or two later my mum passed Charlene to my dad with tears in her eyes.

"What's wrong?" my dad asked.

My mum shook her head. "Nothing, but just take her. She's beautiful."

My dad held Charlie tight and after a moment he also seemed to go into a small trance. Coming back around he stared at my mum with glassy eyes.

"What's wrong?" I sat up concerned, ready to leap out of bed. "Tell me what's going on."

"Did you get them too?" my mum asked my dad, and he nodded.

Mum turned to me. "Shelley, I can't explain it, but while I held Charlene, I received mental images of you as a small child. Happy ones."

"I got the same," my father said.

"But... how?" I stared at my baby.

"I don't know." My mum wiped a tear that had run down her cheek. "Shelley, this baby is the most blessed child

I have ever known. She's only a few hours old and already displaying her gifts of peace."

"Take that those mothers who show off their kid was born with a tooth," I joked, though I had to admit to being a little freaked out by what had just happened. My parents' visit was interrupted when a commotion broke out downstairs, and we strained to hear who the voices belonged to. I could just make out Ebony and Mary's exasperated tones and then I knew who was here. Footsteps sounded on the stairs and without so much as a polite knock on the door, my bestie walked in.

"Shelley, my girl. Where's this new girl in your life who has come to usurp my place of favourite female?" She cast her eyes down onto my mum's lap.

"Oh wow, she is beyond cute. Beyond."

"Kim, can you keep your voice down? She's been really well behaved so far. I don't want you setting her off crying."

Kim looked at me as if I was the one out of order, "I'm this girl's Auntie Kim. She's my girl. I'm going to lead her astray let me tell you." She looked down at the baby. "You come see me when your mummy says you can't have your ears pierced, hair dyed, tattoos, or go to the family planning clinic underage, okay, sweetie?"

My dad shook his head and stood. "We're going to get going, darling. We'll leave you to talk to your friend in peace."

"Peace. You have met Kim, haven't you?"

My mum passed Charlie to Kim and then came over and topped up the glass of water I had by the bed. "You need anything else before I go, darling?"

"No, Mum. I'm fine. Thank you for visiting. You too,

Dad." They kissed me and then Charlie's forehead, before saying farewell to Kim.

"How was it? Your pussy ruined forever?"

"Nope. Vampire healing power. Everything down there is A-okay. I feel absolutely fine."

Kim paused, looking me up and down. "Then why are you in bed?"

"Because I'm playing the exhausted new mother card and if you tell anyone I will drain you."

"Yeah? I'll bite your throat out before you get near me, biatch. Ow." Kim looked down. "Erm, I was stroking your baby's cute mouth and she bit me." She waved her finger in the air where a drop of blood appeared.

"How can she have bit you when she doesn't have a tooth yet?" I beckoned for Kim to pass her over and then I ran my finger over Charlie's gum and felt a canine. What had I just been saying about mothers and their kid's teeth? Looked like someone was getting her vampire fangs already. "Oh, she grew a tooth already. I'm going to feed you now, Charlie. Please don't bite through my nipple." Luckily, she settled at my breast.

"First time I've seen you flash them sober."

"Ha ha. How's married life? Don't think I've forgotten that in my hour of need, you choose an hour of seed."

"It was my wedding night. We had to keep doing it over and over to cement my turning into a were."

I stared at her for a beat. "That's not true, is it?"

She shrugged her shoulders. "No. I'm sorry. I was mesmerised by Darius' cock and by wild kinky wolf sex. As soon as I woke today, I came straight over."

"It's ten past two in the afternoon."

"And I just woke at half one after all the wedding night and wild kinky wolf sex."

"I don't want to know about you doing it as a wolf." I shuddered.

"Right back at you. You're the one who chose to shag a dead guy. Perve."

"Yeah, you make a good point."

Kim stood up and drank down my water. "Gosh, didn't realise how thirsty I was, must be from the wild kinky wolf sex."

"You going to keep saying that? By the way, that was my drink."

"Eboonnnyy. Maryyyy," Kim shouted.

Footsteps ran up the stairs. "Yes. Is there a problem?" Ebony said.

"Yeah, you've let the new mother run out of liquids and not offered her guest a drink. Not good enough, Ebs, not good enough."

Ebony took my glass. "Sorry, Shelley. Water or blood?"

"She's feeding so could I possibly have half and half?"

"Of course."

"Glass of wine for me. Wet the baby's head," Kim said. Then she raised a hand towards Ebony. "Oh and by the way. I wanted to ask you about your vision, Ebs."

"What vision?" I asked with a frown.

"Ebony had a vision of *herself*, in a wedding dress. I was there as a bridesmaid, but she couldn't see the groom."

"I think you just had a nightmare, Ebs, if you'd asked Kim to be a bridesmaid."

"It did cross my mind that it may just be a hallucination and the visions had taken me over to crazyland at long last, but no, it felt like a vision. Though it has faded. Thank you for asking after me, Kim. I've not had anything further."

"I just wondered what my bridesmaid dress looked like," Kim said. "Only I've watched *27 dresses,* and it's made me kind of worried. You are a bit weird after all."

"I'll go get your drinks," Ebony said, excusing herself and leaving the room.

"I'm not a psychic but I foretell you getting the bottle of wine being stuck somewhere the sun doesn't shine if you're not careful," I told my friend.

Kim just grinned. She had no filter and didn't care.

"I'm going to forego my honeymoon, being the extremely kind woman I am, then I can cover your maternity leave from Monday."

"You decided to get married on Thursday, while I was being turned into a vampire in a clinic. There is no honeymoon leave approved."

"I got Lucy to book it on the system, then unbook it, so it's in black and white. Well, actually the computer is in colour, but you get the picture."

"God, you are infuriating."

"So, anyway, you're welcome."

"Gee, thanks."

"Hey, look. Your maternity leave wasn't due to start yet either."

"Kim, you are an amazing person and best friend. Please could you oversee the business while I'm on maternity leave? If the business *runs smoothly* and brings in a *decent income* over the coming weeks, then you may receive a bonus payment."

"Whoop." She did a little jiggle. "Me and Lucy are going to rock this."

I stared at my baby, reminding myself of why I was having maternity leave, so I didn't head into a meltdown and rush back to work. A newly turned werewolf with no filter; and an ex-demon, turned earth-angel, currently on leave from angel duties, with again NO FILTER were running my agency. It was going to go under.

Look at the baby.

Look at the baby.

"I wonder what will happen at Jax's now that she's lost Seth? Do you think business will slow down?"

"Undoubtedly," I replied. "But her coffee and baked goods are exceptional, so I think she'll still have a steady supply of customers off the back of it." Seth had been a good-looking guy who'd worked at our friend's coffee shop as a barista, but he'd been being blackmailed and was the one who had drugged Ebony, making her lose her visions. He'd also added a potion to half the coffee shop customer's drinks in order they kept returning. All to keep him in a job where he could keep an eye on Kim for Jett, the rogue were who had recently been killed along with his mother.

"I'll be happy for it to be quieter. Good job her coffee and doughnuts are to die for because after my recent experiences I might be tempted to go back to making a flask."

I side-eyed her and she fell about laughing.

"I don't know how you can lie like that and keep a straight face."

Feeding over, I burped the baby and passed her back to Kim.

"She is scrumptious, Shelley." She looked down at her,

smiling. "I already love you very, very much," she cooed. "You are the most beautiful baby in the whole wide world. The whole universe."

And that's why she was my best friend. Because even though she was a gob-on-a-stick she loved me and my baby hard.

"Well of course, you are the most beautiful baby until I'm stupid enough to have one," she added, ruining the tender moment.

Charlie gave her own response by throwing up down Kim's white blouse. A heady pink mix all down her chest.

Kim passed her back. "I'm just going to the bathroom to clean up, and that shows you just how much I love you, Charlene Kimberly Landry because I don't even mind you ruined my DKNY blouse."

She left the room.

"Did you hear that, baby girl? I hope you and your daddy are okay with your middle name being Kimberly because we'd not actually spoken about the rest of your name yet with you coming so fast, but I get the feeling your Auntie Kim is kind of convinced we did."

Charlie did the wind smile, and I decided she'd agreed. Now I just had to ask Theo. Actually, it was pretty much a done deal after the whole 'name your baby after a *Neighbour's* character' debacle.

CHAPTER 5

I'd been accepted at the farm as an extra pair of hands and to help ensure the baby stayed safe. I should have been back at work tomorrow, but it looked like the boutique would have to close for a week or two, just while things settled here. Though I loved my shop, the truth was I didn't need the money. I had a decent inheritance, though I'd have rather still had my own mum. Seeing Shelley with the baby was unearthing feelings I'd made my peace with a long time ago. But I still missed my mum.

My mum had been a seer too, and she'd had the boutique before me. When Shelley's parents had first got together, my mum had let them stay in the flat above the shop. The flat that was now the dating agency premises. Unfortunately, one night, Lucy—the woman Dylan had dumped for Shelley's mum, Margret—came to the building where she was coerced by the Devil. A fire followed, the result of which was Dylan and Lucy went to Hell, Margret into exile, and my mum, Yolanda perished in the blaze.

I'd been sent to live with my grandparents. Having

never known my father or anything about him, my maternal grandparents were everything to me and I still visited my grandmother frequently. My grandfather had passed on a couple of years ago. My grandmother mourned him and then moved into a home where she enjoyed the company of the other residents. She lived in London and I didn't get to see her as much as I would have liked.

The shop and apartment above had passed to me and for a long while I'd rented it out, but then my visions had increased, and I'd received a gut feeling that my place was back in Withernsea, doing what my mother had done: running a boutique, and telling people of my visions. I'd continued to rent out the space upstairs as I couldn't bring myself to live where my mum had breathed her last. Then Shelley had turned up one day when Kim had brought her to Jax's coffee shop after meeting her at a speed dating event. They'd had no romance luck but found a new best friend each. My visions had shown her future with Theo and with the dating agency.

My mother didn't communicate with me, but I always had the feeling she was around. It could have been in my head, but in any case I liked to think she was watching me and keeping an eye on things.

This morning our friend Samara who owned the local pet grooming salon had visited Charlene, along with her husband. Theo was asleep in bed and Jax was due this evening.

I walked into Shelley's bedroom. "Okay, why don't you go take a shower while I have Charlene? Then let's get you downstairs shall we, before you begin to fester?"

Shelley pouted. "But I've been enjoying a rest."

"You can still rest downstairs. Now get out of bed."

She huffed but did as she was told. "God, Ebs, you're such a nag bag."

"You can call me what you like, darling. You're still going to wash yourself so that birds don't come nest on your head. Then you can put on clean clothes because this." I cast my hand in the direction of her body. "Is not yummy mummy worthy."

"I just had a baby," Shelley protested.

"Yes, you didn't die, so the corpse look needs to move along."

She grabbed her robe and left to go in the shower. It took barely any time to look presentable. There was no excuse for her not brushing her hair. I stared at Charlene in her crib. "Mummy has gone to get clean, baby girl. Now you won't have to smell her body odour. You're welcome."

I waited for the baby to talk in my mind, but she stayed asleep. Perhaps I'd imagined the whole thing anyway. The visions kept me one step away from a psychiatric unit. I laughed at myself. As if a baby spoke to me. Honestly, Ebony, you're an idiot.

No you're not, but I'm trying to sleep here.

My eyes widened. It wasn't my imagination after all.

"You were right, Ebs, I feel much better for being downstairs. Much more myself, and look, I'm back in my comfy jogging pants already."

"Yay," I said, knowing my expression was pained because comfy jogging pants didn't cut it when you owned a boutique. I'd have to go get her some designer loungewear when I got a spare moment to visit the shop. It could be a 'push present'. Yes, usually, such gifts came from the father, but I needed to save Shelley from becoming the mother who nipped to the shops in her onesie.

Theo was up now and looking very rested. He was on the sofa snuggling with Charlene. Theo always wore a shirt and tie with smart trousers.

"The strangest thing happened yesterday," Shelley announced. "I've been thinking about it, trying to work out how it's possible, but I thought I'd run it past you, Ebs."

"Okay."

"My mum and dad visited as you know and they were upset because they didn't get to raise me. They held Charlie and then both of them received memories of when I was a child. Just a few happy ones."

"Wow," I said, looking over at Charlene. "You really do have one special daughter there."

"Did she really do that? Is a baby capable of such things?"

I sat back on my seat. "We don't know what Charlene will be capable of. Just that she's going to be a very powerful person. But maybe she's inherited all your memories and her father's? Then she's passed those couple of memories on to your own parents?"

Spot on, Ebs.

This is very disconcerting, you speaking in my mind.

How do you think I feel trapped in a baby's body right now? Not in control of my poop. It's very embarrassing. Now carry on, you're reassuring my mum.

38

"I think you could be right. It was such a lovely thing. My parents were ecstatic to see me as a child like that. My mum said Charlie was already bringing peace."

"Yes, I believe that's exactly what she was doing. She's going to be an amazing woman."

The telephone rang, and we heard Mary answer it.

The vision came into my mind but there was no pain.

My first visitor. An important one.

"Are you okay, Ebs? Your eyes rolled white, but you didn't go grey or clutch your head?"

"My visions seem to be changing. They're coming without pain. I wonder if your daughter is helping me too?"

You got it.

Thank you. If you can make my visions pain free, then my gratitude is beyond what I can express in words.

I can sense it from you, words aren't needed.

"What is it, Ebony? What have you seen?"

"Tomorrow, as well as your parents visiting, you are going to be visited by the current Duke of Wyvern Sea, your keeper of the water. He will be bringing his son. They want to talk about your official coronation."

"Oh, that's all I need right now."

"The Duke will make you an offer that you need to turn down. That's all I can tell you. You must turn it down, although at first it will cause friction."

"I'm going to meet him and piss him off. Fab."

"All will progress as it should."

"And you can't tell me anymore?"

"That's all I see. I see him here at the house and he is

frustrated at being turned down for something. But the voices tell me it has to be this way."

"Thank you, Ebony."

Mary came in. "That was some guy's secretary on the phone. Said his name was Brishon Duke, and he and his son Drake Lord wanted to visit tomorrow. They were insistent at coming at eleven even though that's when your parents are coming. You might want to ring back and change it?"

I shook my head at Shelley.

"No, eleven is fine. It seems my human parents and sister are going to mix with the royalty of the seas. This should be interesting."

The doorbell rang. "A woman's work is never done," Mary complained.

"Sit, Mother, and take Charlene for a couple of minutes before Jax wants a squish. I have some business to attend to."

Shelley cocked her head at him. "What business?"

"Nothing for you to worry about, wife. You take charge of the child rearing, and I will supervise the rest of the household."

"Theo, we've spoke about equality how many times now?"

"Do you want me to cuddle Charlie while you discuss supporting walls?"

Shelley sat back. "Enjoy running the household, sweetpea."

Our friend Jax walked in the room clutching a jar of her amazing coffee. "I thought you might be missing this." She passed it to Shelley.

"You're the best. I'm going to make one straightaway. What can I get you to drink?"

"I'll just have a water," Jax said and then she said hello to Mary and cooed at the baby. Mary was not giving her up. Instead, she tightened her grip around her.

"Hello, little Charlene. Aren't you gorgeous? I'm Jax and I've come to meet you and hopefully get a little cuddle with you while I'm here," she hinted.

"My cuddles are keeping her content. We don't want her disturbing now do we?"

Disappointment flashed across Jax's face. "I guess not." She came and sat down on the sofa beside me.

"How's business?"

"It was quiet yesterday, but I decided I'm going to advertise for a new barista. And I'm going to choose another sexy one, Ebs. I don't care about employment regulations. I'll just make it look like I followed them. Hot guy equals more business, so end of debate."

Shelley walked back into the living room followed by Theo; and Jax's brother, Henry, who I hadn't realised had come along. Then I thought of what Theo had said about supporting walls. Henry must be doing some farm refurbishment.

"Oh, hello, Ebony." I knew Henry thought I was a complete fruit loop, but I thought he was an idiot, so it didn't matter.

"Henry," I said coolly.

Jax introduced him to Mary who at that moment was in solid form. Neither Jax nor Henry knew about supernaturals, so they believed Shelley had been further along than she'd first thought in her pregnancy, and that Mary was their nanny. Personally, I'd have liked to out us all to Henry to watch his cocky face turn pale when faced with vampires, ghosts, and seers.

You'll get your chance. Don't worry.

Charlene had woken up.

Fuck, I can't cope with this continual pissing myself.

She started wailing. "Ooh, Charlie. Let me go change your nappy and then Jax can have a cuddle." Shelley took the baby from Mary.

Jax looked delighted. Mary looked annoyed and got up and flounced out.

"The nanny is awfully clingy isn't she?" Henry said. "She dresses weird too. Like someone from years ago. Where'd you get her from, Theo?"

Theo huffed. "She came highly recommended actually, and she's brilliant with the baby."

"Sorry, mate," Henry said with a raised eyebrow.

After a minute of uncomfortable silence Henry spoke again. "I brought my tape measure so am I okay to go do my measurements, ready for getting started tomorrow?"

"Theo, can I have a word, just outside the door please?" Shelley said, coming back in. She passed the baby to Jax. "We'll just be outside. You can be cuddling Charlie.

"I was hoping Theo could show me around the upstairs again..."

"Ebony will take you upstairs, won't you, Ebs?" Shelley's expression showed me I had no choice.

"Women are always wanting to take me upstairs," Henry quipped.

I rolled my eyes as I stood there. Henry was attractive. He had ginger hair and a ginger beard. He'd been mocked at school apparently for being a ginge, whereas his younger sister had taken after their mum and was dark haired. But he had lovely blue eyes and once he'd got over the awkward teenage years, help from the gym had resulted in a buff toned bod, and he'd been fighting women off. I took his attitude to be a cover up of his insecurities of years spent being called 'carrot top' and 'Duracell'.

I led him up the stairs and began with the first room I knew Theo wanted to get refurbished. The farm was going to become a bed and breakfast that he was going to run. Events in Withernsea seemed to keep interfering with his plans, but it looked like he was pushing ahead regardless of the newborn, hence Shelley wanting a 'word'. I'd bet they were ones where she'd need to donate to the swear jar.

"Are you still here from when you collapsed in the coffee shop, Ebony? Because I'm not being funny, but I think Theo and Shelley might want some private time and space with the baby."

"I'm helping out."

"But they already have a nanny."

"I need to be here."

"Oh God. Is this more of your psychic shit?"

My hands automatically went to my hips, and I narrowed my eyes in his direction. "I beg your pardon? I'm not going to explain myself to the likes of you. It's all just wasted words anyway. Believe what you want to believe. I need to be here right now, and I am, so get your measurements and then you can go."

"I'll be back tomorrow. See, I need to be here too."

God he was an arrogant idiot.

Then it came. A vision.

I saw Henry sitting in a restaurant waiting for someone. He was dressed up in smart trousers and a smart shirt, rather than the jeans with frayed knees and paint splattered t-shirt he was wearing now. I watched as the restaurant went dark, showing me that time was passing. He looked at his phone and then at a text, scowled, threw money on the table and then left. The scent of his aftershave came to me both from the vision and from him in the room. As I opened my eyes, I realised he was right next to me.

"Your eyes did that weird arse thing. Is it some kind of fit? Do you need a chair?"

"No, I'm fine." I watched as Henry recorded measurements on an iPad. Rather than use a tape measure he just walked from wall to wall with a device that kept beeping. Another one was used to run down the walls.

"Times have changed since I last decorated it would appear. What are all these things?"

"This records the measurements of the room. It's digital. This checks for wiring behind the walls, and I record everything on my iPad because it looks better than a paper and pen, although secretly I quite like paper, and a pen behind my ear."

This was the first time I think we'd ever had a hint of a normal conversation. Not that I'd met him often, but sometimes he'd visited the coffee shop to see his sister, and she spoke about him enough that I felt I knew him. The last I'd heard he'd had a steady girlfriend of the last two years called Callie.

"So, you still seeing Callie?"

"'Fraid so, babes, so you're shit out of luck if you're trying to check if I'm single."

"Ugh." I grimaced. "No, that's not what I was enquiring about. You're far too uncouth for me, and arrogant."

"You're such a snob. Just because I don't talk in your very posh accent, yar-yar-yar. You think you're better than me. Well, you aren't."

"I don't think I'm better than you. I'm just saying I wouldn't be interested in you in a romantic sense because you say really crude things a lot."

"Like what?"

"Like 'shit'."

"You have a problem with me because I say the word 'shit'?"

"That amongst other things."

He shook his head, widened his eyes, and sighed. "I don't have time for this shit."

"See!"

He started measuring again.

"Are you doing anything nice tonight?" I asked as another way into discussing the contents of my vision.

He turned to me, his forehead creasing. "If you're fishing about when I'll be leaving, then yes, it will be soon. I'm meeting Callie at Beached."

"And you've not had a text from her at all, about her cancelling?"

He rubbed his forehead.

"Why would I have a text from her cancelling? She's been pestering for me to take her for weeks. In fact, that's all she ever wants to do. Go to that bloody restaurant. It's costing me a fortune."

"I was just wondering."

"Oh God. Don't tell me you've had a bloody vision about it because I'm not into believing any of that bollocks. Now find something else to do because a) you're weird, and b) you're acting even weirder than usual.

"Sorry, I spoke. I was only trying to help you."

"You're the one needs help from where I'm standing. Right, I'm ready to see the other rooms. I think I got this now. You can go. I'll be quicker if you're not rambling and getting on my nerves."

"It was lovely seeing you too, Henry." I smiled with a complete look of smug satisfaction in my eyes. "Enjoy your evening."

Returning downstairs, I headed for the kitchen. I made myself a coffee, sneaking a spoonful of Jax's gift. I needed some of her amazing nectar of the gods. How come morons like Henry got dates, but I found it difficult? Men always ran away the first time my eyes rolled in my head. I told them I had epilepsy, but the grey pallor had made me look corpse-like and I think they genuinely thought their date might die on them.

Looking at Shelley and Kim had made me question my own future. They were both happily married now. I wanted some romance in my life and maybe if my visions were going to be less painful and my pallor less grey from now on, then I wouldn't be as scary a prospect?

A shooting pain passed through my temple. Nowhere near what I'd had before, but the first pain I'd had since being at the farm. I put a hand to my forehead.

There I was again in church. I looked down at myself and there was my dress. White, plain. I looked behind me and I could see my train.

Shelley stood behind me in a pale blue satin bridesmaid dress. "We can't go in there yet. The groom hasn't arrived."

The vision ended.

"You really need to get that checked out. All that eye-rolling can't be doing you any good."

Sitting down at the kitchen table, I reached for a jotter pad and a pen that Shelley used for shopping lists. I ignored Henry and wrote everything down, every word, just in case it all faded again.

I looked up at him as I could feel his eyes staring at me.

"Seriously, are you okay?"

"I'm fine. Just feeling a bit tired. Babies, you know," I lied. "You were quick."

"Yeah, once you were out of my hair not yapping anymore, I got things down in next to no time. Right, I'm off on my hot date. I'll be back at nine am. Have the kettle on hot won't you and keep continual cups of tea coming?"

I bit on my lower lip to stop me from saying things I'd regret.

"Thanks, Ebs," he said, using my nickname that he had certainly not earned the right to use. "You're the shit." And then he strode back out of the kitchen.

Sitting back in my chair, I took a deep breath and picked up the hot drink, taking a sip of the dark aromatic liquid. Perhaps I'd need my vodka back. Not for any potential vision headaches but just to stop me from killing Henry Marston. Right there and then I vowed that no matter what visions I had regarding Henry, unless I needed to warn him of impending death, I was telling him nothing. I'd tried to warn him about his date and just received insults in return. I'd keep any and all information to myself and let him experience every hiccough that would befall him.

In the meantime, tomorrow I was going to pop out and over to see Kim and Lucy at the dating agency. Because my husband was out there somewhere, and I needed to meet him. What better way than joining the dating agency I'd helped get started in the first place? I'd have Kim in my debt anyway. Because I now could tell her what her bridesmaid dress looked like, and it was gorgeous.

CHAPTER 6

EBONY

"Y ou want to join the dating agency?" Kim gave me a look of disbelief. "But you've had a vision you were getting married anyway so what's the point?"

Lucy threw a paperclip at her. "We don't turn down customers, dumb ass. I'm opening the application form online as we speak," she said.

"We can't ask Ebs to pay. She's one of the main reasons the dating agency exists," Kim moaned. "We'd be working for free."

"God, I wish I could still shoot flames out of my fingers so I could fire one under your lazy ass. Sorry, Ebony. Kim is having far too much sex at the moment and because she doesn't have a healthy diet, she's tired all the time. Whereas me and Frankie are at it like rabbits, so I eat lots more fruit and veg, especially carrots. Rabbits, carrots. You get it?" She giggled.

"Bring back the bloody demon," Kim groaned. "Your jokes are worse than anything you did in Hell."

Lucy looked at me and bit her lip and I knew what she

was thinking. No matter the circumstances, her actions had led to the death of my mother.

"Application form opened. Right, Ebony. Can you tell me your full name, please?"

"Ebony Yolanda Walker."

Lucy carried on recording my personal details including my address and family history.

"Okay, let's get onto potential ideal date questions. What's your favourite food?"

"Caviar and smoked salmon blinis accompanied by a lovely glass of champagne."

"Erm, okay. And would Prosecco and a fish finger sandwich do at a push?"

"I suppose."

"Ideal dating venue?"

I sucked on my top lip for a moment. "Theatre, day at the races, high tea. Anything like that."

Kim looked at Lucy and burst into a fit of laughter. "Glad you agreed to take her on now? Good luck with getting her a date. It's Withernsea not Windsor."

Lucy sighed. "Okay, if you could take a moment now to fill in this part of the application form for me. I'll input it into the computer afterwards." She passed me the sheet attached to a clipboard, along with a pen.

I looked down at it, *Reason for Application*. I began.

For the past few years I have been so troubled with visions that I did not believe romance was indeed part of my future. However recent visions have shown me that I am to be married at some point though I know not to whom. Therefore,

I would like to actively seek out romantic encounters so that I might learn who my future intended is.

My visions are currently coming without pain and I am not having to consume my usual copious amounts of vodka which could render me unable to speak properly on a date. Thus it is an ideal time for me to look for a partner.

Thank you for considering my application.

I handed it over to Lucy who began to type it in. "Your visions are coming without pain? That must be a relief?"

"It really is. I feel like I'm getting to be me."

Lucy smiled. "That's wonderful, Ebony."

Kim tilted her head at me. "You know your visions, Ebs?"

"Yes."

"You don't actually see yourself married in them, do you? You're just standing in a wedding dress."

I thought back. It was true. In fact in my most recent vision, my intended was missing.

"Err, yes, that's correct."

"Maybe you get jilted, Ebs. We have to consider the possibility that the groom either doesn't show or is a result of an hallucination from too much vodka."

"Kim! You've gone too far," Lucy yelled.

"I'm just looking out for my friend. She needs to not focus so much on her vision and start living her life now she's pain free."

"I see what you're getting at, Kim, although it's delivered in your usual delicate flower like way."

Lucy snorted.

"Go on these dates to enjoy yourself, Ebs. Not to question if every single one is your future husband. That's all I'm saying."

"Be free, single, and ready to mingle." I winked at her.

"You got it, babes. Now go book in at a beauty salon and get everything freshened up."

"I already am 'freshened up'. It's part of my routine to look elegant *everywhere* at all times."

"Bare, hair, or landing strip there? Personally, I rate a landing strip so they know where they're aiming for." Kim stood, motioning with her arms like an air hostess. "Please take note of the areas here, here, and here."

"I take it this is not part of the official application form?" I said to Lucy.

Lucy shook her head. "You know that vodka you don't need any more, Ebony...?"

"It's behind my shop counter whenever you need it." I rose from my seat. "Thank you, ladies. It's been... interesting. I shall look forward to seeing whomever the computer matches me up with."

"I'll be in touch shortly about your first date," Lucy said.

"Right, I'd better get back to the farm because there are a lot of visitors due to arrive at eleven."

"Oh yes, could you give Shelley this card and present from me and tell her I'd love to visit but I'll need to make sure her mum and dad aren't going to be around. It could be a little awkward."

"Sure."

"Oh yeah, her adoptive parents are visiting today, aren't they?" Kim suddenly remembered.

"Yes, and the Duke of Wyvern Sea and his son."

"Hey, how old are they? Maybe one of them is your future husband, Ebs?"

A slow smile crept across my face. *Not mine, Kim. Not mine.*

I returned to the house and went to fix myself a drink. All that talking had proved to be thirsty work. I really ought to have called in at the coffee shop, but time was passing quickly. Unfortunately, Henry also happened to be in the kitchen, Mary at his side. "Please be careful with the cups, Henry. Some have been in the family for years. We don't want chips." She turned to me. "Oh fantastic. Please can you educate Henry here on the importance of fine china, Ebony? Only I must dash." Her body went a little translucent, and she left the room before Henry could notice.

"Thought you were going to be here to make my drinks? Then I wouldn't need to be having my every move watched. I'm quite okay with this mug but she even kicked off about me using that." He pointed to a mug that said *This isn't coffee* with blood splatters on the front.

"Oh that was a gift from Theo to Shelley." I picked it up and placed it back in the cupboard. "Here, use this one." I passed him an orange mug.

"Have you automatically gone for that because I'm ginger?" He raised a brow. Then placing his mug next to the kettle, he went in the cupboard rummaging and brought out a black mug which he passed to me. "Here you are."

"You're such a child. I don't know why I bothered to

try to help you." Filling up the kettle, I switched it on and then I remembered my vision.

I rested back against the worktop. "Did you have a nice time at Beached the other night?"

The skin around Henry's eyes bunched, and he rubbed the back of his neck. I noted his hands clenched into fists. "Not exactly."

"Oh. Sorry." I busied myself putting coffee in my cup. "Tea for you?" I asked him.

"Yes please. Strong, one sugar, plenty of milk."

There was silence as we waited for the kettle to boil.

"She didn't show and then I got a text while I was there. She dumped me by text." He shook his head. "Two years and that's what I was worth. And do you know why she'd wanted to go to Beached? Because she was shagging one of the bar staff there. Had been for the last six months. She wanted me to meet her there so she could show him what he was missing by not committing to her. Except he did. He proposed. So it was bye bye, Henry."

"I'm sorry, Henry."

His expression changed, becoming guarded. "Anyway, it was nothing to do with your psychic shit. Just that she was a cheating bitch. Best thing is, I'd been thinking of dumping her for ages. Things were stale."

"Maybe that's why she did what she did? Though I don't condone cheating." I'd switched the kettle off just before it boiled, adding water to my mug and then flicked it back on.

"Why'd you do that?" He pointed to my mug.

"Coffee is better if it's almost boiled, not completely."

He huffed. "Thought you'd be drinking Earl Grey from a china teacup."

I bristled. "Yes, I like nice things and I was brought up around money, but I've worked in my boutique for years now. I'm not some pampered princess." I shoved his mug towards him. "The kettle's boiled, make your own tea, because you're no Prince Charming either."

I stormed out of the kitchen. God that man. How had Jax put up with being his younger sister? I'd bet he used to push her off swings and chase her with spiders and frogs. Anyway, I had much more important things to do than make tea for that imbecile. The visitors were due any moment. I made my way to my room to freshen up before they all arrived.

"Ebony! You're back," I announced very obviously as she walked into the living room. "Thank goodness for that, only I'm feeling extremely fatigued, and Mary is fading in and out. Could you receive the visitors while I go nap?"

She gave me some serious side-eye. "You hardly sleep anymore, and there's no way I'm being left with your visitors. Now as they say in your world, 'Grow a pair'."

"They say that in your world too, Ebs. You live in Withernsea now. It's okay to adapt and to adopt some of the local dialect."

"Shut yer mouth, stop talking shit, and get ready to look pleased to see the old folk," Ebony said, trying to adopt a local accent, but it came out, *'shoot yerrr mouth, stop talking shite, and get ready to luke pleased to seee the owlde fowk'.*

She shrugged. "I tried."

"This... my adoptive parents and this bloke from the sea

coming. It's worse than childbirth. I dread to think what's going to happen."

Ebony crossed one leg over the other. "What will happen is whatever destiny has planned, Shelley. It will happen whether you dread it or not."

This was where I wanted Kim. Ebony was no good to just plain whinge at. It was always: *because it's fate.* Oh blah, blah, bloody blah.

The doorbell rang and Ebony rose. "I'll go receive the visitors while you prepare yourself for the inevitable."

Yeah thanks.

My adoptive parents had arrived. I'd had to perform a spell on myself to keep my amusement under control because I knew I'd have a hard time not giggling at their actions. I'd seen enough of it at our wedding. Mark and Debbie (I'd largely stopped calling them mum and dad as they'd never acted like proper parents), walked in as if the floor was filled with booby traps and the air with those red laser beams they used to protect jewels. Finally, they managed to get as far as the sofa.

"Hey. Take a seat."

Polly came through the door a minute after them, but she didn't pause, she just walked straight through. "Sorry, I was just parking the car, only there are paint pots everywhere."

Ebony huffed, a disgusted look coming over her face. "I do apologise. It's the decorator, Henry. He has no idea about tidiness or the fact there are other people to consider."

"I can hear you," a voice bellowed down the stairs.

"Good," she shouted back up.

Oh dear.

Feet trampled down the stairs and Henry stuck his head in the room. He took one look at my pretty blonde younger sister and straightened his posture, a smile replacing his frown.

"Sorry for any inconvenience caused. I'll go tidy up right now. Do you need to move your vehicle?"

Polly shook her head. "No, it's fine now thanks."

"Oh, well I'll go tidy up out there anyway ready for when you leave."

Ebony cleared her throat. I looked over, watching as her eyes went white.

My parents gasped and grasped each other.

A second or two later Ebony's sight returned to normal, and she cackled with laughter. She looked like a madwoman.

"Ebony's a seer, remember? Is everything okay there, Ebs?"

"Absolutely wonderful." Ebony smiled. "Just so nice to see Henry take such an interest in Polly here. He's about to have an interesting encounter with another 'bird'."

Polly shifted uncomfortably on her seat.

I looked at my parents and Polly. All three of them had made sure they were warded before they came here. They still didn't seem to grasp the fact that I could tear their wards and protection spells down in seconds. I had to remind myself that it was a lot to ask for them to accept all the supernatural aspects of my existence. I stared down at my daughter and whispered, "Please don't do your eye change thing."

"What was that?" Mark said.

"I was just saying to Charlie please don't need changing. I want her to behave for her grandma and grandad. You're okay to be called that, aren't you?"

My adoptive dad looked at my mum, who nodded her head. "Yes, we'd like that very much."

I was sure once the golden child had dropped a sprog, Charlie wouldn't get a look in, but seeing as she had an extended supernatural family and would rule Withernsea, I was sure she'd not give too much of a damn. That was the hope anyway. If these three hurt my daughter in any way I'd turn them into toads.

"Would you like to hold her?" I asked Polly, deciding that as she was the calmest of the three, she could reassure my parents that they weren't going to be killed by the baby.

"Is Theo not around?" Debbie asked.

"He'll be in bed, Debbie, remember? He's a vampire."

"Oh yes of course," she said, facepalming her forehead.

I passed Charlie over to Polly who instantly began cooing over her.

"Oh, that's something I meant to tell you. I'm also a vampire now. I got turned a few days before Charlie was born."

Polly stilled. My parents leaped behind the sofa. I just sat there with my mouth hanging open. Ebony rolled her eyes at me.

"I do not foresee you coming to any harm with Shelley." Ebony looked over the back of the sofa. "It is quite safe to come out."

Slowly, they made their way back to the sofa, straightening their clothes as they did so.

"Arrrrgh, for fuck's sake. Stupid birds." The door

banged and Henry lumbered through. "Shelley, sorry to inconvenience you, but would I be able to take a shower? I was standing under the gutters and a bird decided to take a poop. It's gone everywhere."

"That's supposed to be lucky," Ebony said, with a shit-eating grin on her face.

Henry glared at her. I was going to need to keep these two apart. They absolutely hated one another.

"Yes, of course. You know where the bathroom is and there are spare towels in the cupboard in there. Use what you need."

Red faced, whether through anger or embarrassment, Henry left the room and went upstairs.

"You have the decorator in?" Debbie enquired.

"Yes, he's doing the spare bedrooms so that Theo can open his bed and breakfast."

She pulled a face. "Do you think it's wise, taking strangers in when you have a child now?"

"It was okay before if they wanted to murder me then?" I quipped.

"You know what your mum's getting at. There are some weird people around, plus thieves. What if someone steals from you?"

"I'll get Kim to scent them down and tear out their throat. She's a werewolf now."

Their eyes widened.

Ebony turned to my parents. "Please excuse my manners. I haven't offered you a drink. Would you like one?"

"Two sherries please," Mark said, despite the fact it was

twenty past eleven in the morning. My mother nodded her head vigorously.

"I thought there were other guests coming?" Polly asked, barely looking up from my daughter's face. "I'm Auntie Polly. Hello, Charlie. I am really good at sports and so if I can help you with any of that when you're older, then just let me know. I'll take your mum's place at sports day if you like because she runs like someone is pushing a pole up her bum. Oh look she's smiling. Is that because Auntie Polly is saying funny things? Pole up bum, pole up bum."

"It's wind," I said a little too fiercely. I took a deep breath. "Yes, the other guests were meant to be here at eleven also. Maybe they changed their minds?" We moved onto talking about Polly's job. She was a PE Teacher and loved it.

A loud hammering on the door indicated new visitors.

"You'd think they'd bear in mind that there could be a baby fast asleep in here," Debbie said.

"You'd think so." For once I was in agreement with her. There was a first time for everything. I'd better ask Lucy if she could check whether or not Hell had frozen over. "But I've never met these people before and I'm unsure of their ways, so we'll see how it goes."

My parents shared a look.

"I have it under control if there's any funny business." I allowed a small amount of blue webs to tingle around my fingertips.

Pained smiles dragged at their lips. "Great," Mark said.

Ebony had left the kitchen to attend to the door. I heard loud voices, then she walked into the room. "I'm just going to finish pouring the sherry. Apparently, it is customary for you to greet the Duke of the Sea yourself and not send one of your servants." She arched a brow.

"I'm sorry, Ebony." Sighing, I got up and went to the entrance where I re-opened the door.

"Greetings," I said, completely over-the-top, taking the piss out of the whole scenario. "Please welcome to my own abode, Duke Brishon and Lord Drake." I curtsied to the elderly portly gentleman at my door, and to his blonde-haired, blue-eyed son who'd let my body know my core wasn't as asleep after childbirth as I'd first thought.

"Oh my goodness, dear lady. You don't curtsy to us. We bow to you." Brishon dipped in an elegant bow, and his son followed.

"Please come in. My human adoptive parents are here, as is my human adoptive sister, and my friend who is a seer. My husband is in bed, and we also have a human decorator in. I thought I'd better let you know who everyone is so you can be prepared. Also, my mother-in-law who's a ghost sometimes appears."

"What a busy household." Drake laughed. Seriously he even sounded like a Disney Prince. I was waiting for Ariel to call at the door next asking for him back.

We wandered into the living room, and I was about to introduce my guests when I realised one of them was missing. I stuck my head back down the hall to see a ghost standing as solid as ever in front of Drake.

"Ah, Drake. This is my mother-in-law, Mary. She's a ghost," I reminded him.

Drake scratched at his temple. "But I thought ghosts were wispy things?"

"She is when she's burned out her energy." I turned to her. "Mary, can you please remember these are our guests?"

"But his hair is very soft and silky."

God help me.

"Mary, do you want me to invent a spell that traps you in one of the bedrooms forevermore?"

She stared down at her feet and mumbled something that sounded a lot like, 'Spoilsport'. I was going to have to talk to Theo about her behaviour. It was getting worse. We couldn't have her molesting all the sexy males who came to the house. She needed a date herself and fast.

"Please, come with me to the living room." I gestured for Drake to follow me.

"We've tried to introduce ourselves, but the gentleman put his hand up and yelled, 'Silence'," Mark said, looking like he wanted to punch Brishon square in the jaw.

I pushed a hand through my hair. Roll on the visits ending so I didn't have all this drama. Then I rethought my sentence. This was my life now. Someone help me.

My daughter made a little gurgling noise and everyone fell silent and turned to look at her. She was such a charmer.

"Okay, introductions." I announced everyone and then Brishon walked over to the crib.

"What a beautiful baby. Now, Shelley, we have business matters to attend to. If I may speak freely?" He gestured to the rest of the people.

"Of course."

"We should have held your coronation by now but seeing as you have given birth to your daughter who will be the true ruler of Withernsea, I thought we might conduct a smaller ceremony here among those assembled, rather than inconvenience a busy new mother. It's a simple ceremony."

"Okay. Sounds good. What do we need to do?" Anything that saved me having to spend a day in the sea faffing around with a 'coronation' and the pomp and ceremony I'd expect from Brishon after his entrance here, was welcomed.

"Could we stand outside?"

"Ah, for a bit of grandeur. Of course. We have a lovely garden with an arbour."

Everyone trailed outside although it was bloody freezing with it being the 12th of February. Oh shit! It was almost Valentine's Day! How come Samara, one of the bloody Cupids of the world, hadn't thought to mention this when she visited? Probably because she liked to pretend it wasn't her job, and it was now mine, the lazy sod! Oh God, I needed to phone Kim. I bet we'd had an influx of applications to the agency. People became increasingly desperate on Valentine's. I shook my head. Focus on the here and now, Shelley. I really needed to do a course on Mindfulness, so I could not look at all the chaos around me and instead focus on what was around me at that particular moment. In this case my coronation.

"I just need a few things from my car. Drake and I will be back shortly."

While they were gone, I tapped my mobile phone until my biological dad's number appeared.

"Hello, love. Is everything okay?"

"Yes, but Dad, I have Brishon and Drake here and they want to perform my coronation right now. Are they trustworthy? Is there anything I need to watch out for?"

"Just make sure you have your usual protection spells in place and you'll be fine. Brishon's a good guy. Full of his own importance but decent all the same, and his son is lovely."

"Thanks, Dad."

"I thought I'd be there to witness the ceremony; be able to wear my jewelled suit." Good Lord, now my dad was giving me grief.

"Yeah, well, you got a granddaughter instead, so the pay-off is her instead of a big ceremony. I tell you what, if I get her christened you can wear your suit then."

I hung up because Brishon and Drake were walking back over carrying a large trunk between them. They set it down on the ground and opened it up.

Inside was a crown. If I'd thought it would be festooned with the jewels of the sea, I was wrong. It was made of a rusted metal and dripped with seaweed.

"If everyone could gather around." Brishon gestured with his hands.

Debbie kept hold of Charlie while I stood in front of Brishon.

"Please kneel."

I lowered myself to the floor, the cold and damp soaking into my jogging bottoms.

"In front of these witnesses here present, I bestow upon Shelley Landry the rule of Wyvern Sea. I grant her access to the waters, and safe passage to her and anyone she may choose to travel alongside her to visit us in the future. All of the sea bows to thee, our new Queen. Do you accept the position? If so, please state now before our assembled guests."

"I accept the position of Queen of Wyvern Sea."

"Drake. If you could please place the crown on our Queen."

The rusting, dripping heap was placed on my head, seaweed going in my eye. I very demurely moved it to one side.

"If everyone present could stand in for the people of the seas and please kneel before our Queen and pledge their allegiance." He pulled me up to standing.

One by one my family and friends had to lower themselves before me as Brishon bossed them into saying they pledged their allegiance. Mark and Debbie said it so quickly and at the same time that I could barely make out the words. I could see that it would be a long while before they visited again, no matter how cute Charlie was. From now on, I was getting invited to theirs. It was written all over their faces. I couldn't blame them. They'd adopted a child and got far more than they'd bargained for. Polly meanwhile was chatting with Drake; they were talking about swimming strokes. Polly had done her lifeguard training and helped run swimming lessons at a local pool. At least one of my human family was embracing the crazy. I'm sure it had nothing to do with him looking like a Disney Prince. I stared at them both. Polly looked like a Disney Princess. If only she could live underwater, they'd have been perfect together. Jesus, I was still matchmaking, even now.

"Okay, one final thing. This is for you." Brishon lifted out a golden coloured box that was intricately painted with pictures of fish. Each one had jewels for eyes. Oooh, a present. Now we were talking. The box was about the size of two shoeboxes. Was it filled with jewellery? I was excited to find out.

"If you could lower yourself towards me, I will do the rest. It shall be my honour," added Brishon. He was definitely pulling out a proper crown and a necklace, and maybe a jewelled staff that folded up to fit in the box. I lowered my head and Brishon opened the box, lifting it and hurtling the contents towards me with force before I had a chance to see and escape. Fish, starfish, shells, seaweed, and dirty sea water coated me from head to foot. I rubbed my eyes.

"And that concludes the ceremony. Let us applaud Queen Shelley of Wyvern Sea."

Everyone slow clapped while trying not to laugh, I could see it in their eyes; except for Brishon and Drake who applauded with enthusiasm.

I could only thank God that Kim wasn't here because there would have been some quip about the Duke having made me wet.

Walking back to the house, Brishon took my arm. "I would like to make a proposal to you, my Queen, if I may?"

Ah, here it came. The very thing Ebony had told me I must turn down.

"Yes, Duke Brishon?"

"I wonder if I may put forward my son Lord Drake as the future intended of Charlene Landry?"

Drake began to choke on his own saliva. "Dad! She's a baby."

"Thank you very much for your kind offer," I said to Brishon. "But Charlene will choose her own suitor when she is of age, by which time I am sure such a wonderful son as yours will have been snapped up by an equally wonderful woman."

"Humph. It's quite rude to so overtly turn down your Duke you know?" I swear the man pouted.

"I am not turning you down. Merely saying Charlene will choose. If your son remains single or you have a grandson in the next year or so, who knows what will happen. But I will not set up my daughter. That is one thing as Queen I will not change my mind on."

"Very well. Drake? It's time for us to leave now. Our business is concluded."

Drake looked at Polly, and Polly looked at Drake.

Brishon was wrong. I didn't think business was concluded at all.

I looked across at Ebony who was also watching the two of them. She gave me an enigmatic smile, and I knew there was a possibility Drake would become family after all.

CHAPTER 8

SHELLEY

I rose early and hit the shower. All night I'd been thinking of Valentine's and the dating agency. I was taking Charlie out. We were off to Jax's and I was calling a business meeting to discuss the days ahead. A quick call to Jax and she agreed to assemble the *Female Entrepreneurs do it with their Colleagues* gang.

I caught up with Ebony in the kitchen, who looked her usual well-maintained gorgeous self. I'd tied my hair up in a ponytail, put a muslin cloth over my shoulder and was dressed in my fave jeans and slouchy t-shirt.

"Ebony, we're off out to Jax's to talk biz. I can't stay in this house a moment longer."

She looked me up and down. "Okay. Pass Charlene to me while you go to get ready."

"I am ready."

"Yes, I knew you were going to say that. Absolutely not. No way." She held up a hand. "Stay there."

I fixed myself some toast and drank an O-neg while her footsteps padded up and down the stairs. I heard Henry moan that she was in his way, and her tell him she was going out and while he had the place to himself he could hopefully finish and get out of the house forever. If this carried on, I was going to have to call a house meeting as I didn't want either of them leaving their current roles.

She stomped back downstairs and returned to the kitchen with clothes draped over her arm.

"I know your figure is exactly as it was before due to the turning, so you can get these snug fitting designer jeans on, along with this blouse. She held up a pink cotton blouse covered in a blue and white butterfly design. Then I'm going to straighten your hair, put some make-up on you, and you are going to revel in all your yummy mummyness in the coffee shop. You are the leader of Withernsea, not one of the winos who hangs around the sea front when the sun goes down."

"Why do I have to get dressed up?"

She pointed to Charlie who I'd dressed in a pretty dress with, damn, flowers and butterflies on it, plus frilly socks. "Same reason you've dressed Charlene up beautifully."

"I hate you," I said, taking the clothes from her arm and passing her Charlie.

Of course, as usual, Ebony had a total amazing eye, and I emerged back downstairs looking and feeling fabulous in the clothes. The denim and the cotton were soft against my skin and the blouse draped enough that you couldn't see my nursing bra underneath. I put on a decent pair of flat shoes and then let Ebony do my hair and make-up. She was in her element and when she'd finished, I almost didn't recognise myself.

"There's no need to let yourself go, just because you've got a husband."

"And it's that snobby attitude which means you don't have one." Henry came through the door and flicked on the kettle after checking there was enough water in it. "You're all presentable, and yet no one goes near you. Maybe you should give that some thought before you dish your advice to other people?"

Ebony swallowed and her eyes went glassy. Henry had hit a nerve. She quickly left the room. I turned to him.

"We're having a house meeting later to get to the bottom of this. You were way out of line there and you upset my friend." He began to speak, and I held up a hand. "I know she says insulting things to you too, and if you want to both carry on like that outside my house, do your worst, but inside my house while you're being paid to work, you will be respectful to the people here. I will be speaking to Ebony this morning too."

He looked at the floor and scuffed one trainer against another. "You're right. I'm sorry, Shelley. There's just something about her rubs me up the wrong way."

"Well, we need to get you two rubbing up together the right way."

His eyes went wide, and I realised what I'd said.

"Oh is that the time? I need to be at Jax's. Excuse me, Henry." I dashed from the room before I said anything else embarrassing.

After spending ten minutes working out getting Charlie in her car seat into the taxi, we were on our way. Ebony had gone quiet.

"Ignore what Henry said. He's just being a dick because of you getting at him. I told him he went too far."

"He was right though. I'm telling you what to look like and you're happily married with a baby. I never let my manicure chip and I have no-one. It only hurt because it was the truth."

"Still, I told him that we're having a house meeting to clear the air. He can apologise."

"He has nothing to apologise for. This time."

"Ignore him. You've seen your wedding anyway in visions, so what does Henry know, eh?" I tried to jolly things up a bit because I'd been excited to get out of the house and now it was like I was in a funeral cortege.

"Kim said that I only actually saw myself at the wedding, and indeed in my second vision I was asking where my groom was. So like she said, I could get jilted at the altar."

I was going to kill Kim when I saw her.

"I joined the dating agency yesterday. Figured it wouldn't hurt to go on some dates. It's been a while. Kim said I should focus on the right now and if it happened, it happened."

Okay, you managed to rescue yourself, Mrs Wild.

As I got out of the taxi, I noticed in the wing mirror that a black car had pulled up a little way down the road. Since having Charlie I'd become more paranoid.

"Ebony, have you had any visions of danger regarding me and Charlie?"

She shook her head. "I'd have told you."

"Do me a favour. Get back in the taxi."

She gave me a weird look but did as asked, and I made

the taxi set off around the local roads. Sure enough, the car started again and followed a way behind.

"We're being tailed." I asked the taxi driver to pull into the Aldi car park. "You take care of Charlie while I go deal," I told Ebs. The taxi driver didn't bat an eyelid. He was a friend of Lucy's and from Angel Cabs.

"Okay."

I parked at the top of the car park and watched as the black car pulled into a space at the opposite end. I muttered an invisibility spell and teleported to the side of the suspect vehicle. Becoming visible again, I made all the doors open, and I sent blue webs out to wrap around anyone in the vehicle.

"Shelley, it's me. Fuck, get these things off me, they tickle."

"Rav, what are you doing following me?" I dropped my webs and looked at Theo's friend who was wearing a guilty expression.

"You're going to be mad. It's better I don't tell you."

"With one spell I can make you tell me, Rav, so c'mon... spill."

"I'm earning a little extra money from Theo. He hired me to be your bodyguard. With me being a demon, he thought I could help if you needed someone while he was asleep."

"He did what? I am perfectly capable of taking care of myself."

"I know. I know. And I told him that, but he wants to feel he's protecting you. You're extremely powerful now, Shelley, and the baby will be too. I think it's threatening his manhood. You need to let him feel you need him. He feels powerless, especially while he has to be asleep all day, whereas you are getting to swan around as usual even though you are part vampire."

"Swan around?" My eyes narrowed.

"I just meant you can go out and he cannot. Just let me do my job and then he can feel better, and I can afford to move out of my mother's house. She keeps going on about how I should be married by now and raising little hellions all over the place. I need some space."

I sighed. "You follow at a distance and don't get in my way. Okay?"

"Yes, yes, absolutely fine. Thank you, Shelley."

I walked back to the taxi shaking my head and then returned to the coffee shop. I was going to consume a bucket full of the stuff.

"A bodyguard. Pahahahahaha." Kim giggled.

"Rav will be a great bodyguard. He does a grand job in Hell," Lucy added.

"The sooner the bed and breakfast opens the better. Then Theo will have something to occupy his time and he can leave me alone."

"Yeah, you have just given birth to his daughter. His first born. Dream on and get used to him breathing down your neck just before he bites it."

"Kim, sod off."

She grinned.

"You had a baby four days ago. There should be laws against you looking so good. But why are you already out of the house and here calling a business meeting? We only took over yesterday. A little faith in us would be good, bestie."

"I just remembered it was Valentine's day tomorrow and wanted to check in with you. I'd forgotten to warn you how mad it gets."

"You do remember I've been here since day one, right?" Kim's jaw had set. "I'm well aware of what happens on Valentine's." She turned to Ebony. "A shit ton more people apply. When I was single, I absolutely loved it, because the men are all desperate. I used to have them eating out of my hand and then eating—"

"Stop right there," I yelled at my best friend. "Everything is in order then?"

She and Lucy nodded. "Yes, all running smoothly."

I sank in my seat. "So I didn't really need to come running?"

"It's good to see you and Charlie again though," Samara said, her blonde curls bouncing as she spoke.

"Are you actually working tomorrow?" I asked her.

"I suppose I'll probably do an hour. They've sent me the latest state-of-the-art bow and arrows. Might as well try them out. But I don't want to take away from your business, so I won't shoot too many."

"That reminds me. Kim, Lucy, I want you to find Mary a date. Is there another ghost hanging around that she could spend some time with?"

"We have a few on the books. I'll have a look. Can she complete an online application as she can't leave the house, can she? Actually, how will she get to her date?" Lucy frowned.

"They'll have to come to her. So she needs one that can move. Make sure he's young and fit, okay?"

"And how does Theo feel about his mother dating again?"

"Yeah, like I've told him. Look, she's feeling the backsides of any men who enter the house, and then half the time she disappears after. If I don't get her a date, she's going to have me sued for harassment."

"Okay. Young, fit, and can travel. I'll look once I leave here."

"Thanks, Lucy."

Jax came over which rendered the supernatural talk over.

"What have I missed?"

"Just cuddles with Charlene, nothing else of importance." I handed my daughter over to her.

"At least your nanny isn't around today to get all possessive about the baby."

"Right." Kim stood up. "We're going to have to make a move because we're really busy with it being the run up to Valentine's. I could rush you a date through, Ebs, if you like?"

"No, I can wait until afterwards."

"Are you sure?"

"Ebony." I pushed her arm. "Go for it."

"Oh, okay. Find me a date for tomorrow evening, but please, not someone desperate."

"Even though they'd be all over an 'all you can eat Ebony buffet'?"

"Especially for that reason. Just a nice, calm individual."

"Can they be human?" Kim blurted out.

"What else are they going to be?" Jax laughed. "You started a new section matching people with pets?"

"There's always a desire for pussy." Kim winked at Jax and then kissed my cheek. "Later, tater. Bye bye, Charlie K."

Jax went back off to serve her customers as she still didn't have a replacement for Seth yet. Samara said her goodbyes and returned to her pet grooming salon, and that left me and Ebony.

"I don't feel needed," I told her. "We might as well just go back home."

"Or we could have a chocolate doughnut," she said, glancing at the counter.

I didn't need much persuading.

Before we returned home, Ebony opened the shop, and I helped her with a few stocktaking tasks while she opened post and made sure everything was okay.

"Ebony?" I looked around.

"Yeah?"

"Have you thought of having an online boutique? That way you could still work while you're at the house. It must be kind of boring just waiting for my visitors to arrive."

"Well, I didn't want to complain as it has only been a few days, but with me missing time here when I was ill also, I'm worried my customers will move elsewhere, and I do love matching people to outfits. I wouldn't know how to start though."

"But Theo is an internet whizz. He'd set you up, I'm sure, if you asked him."

Ebony's face became animated, like she'd had an extra shot of coffee. "Do you think he'd be able to help me with an online 'What would suit you?' style guide type thing?"

"Ebony, please ask him and get him occupied with something other than having me followed. Until the B&B is finished, he's lacking for things to do."

Ebony stared at Charlie for a beat. "Yes, yes. I think that's a fabulous idea," she said.

"Why did you stare at the baby before deciding?"

"Erm, her outfit was just giving me ideas," she replied.

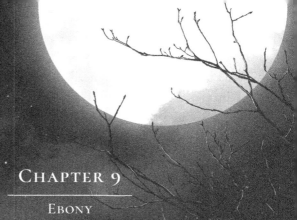

CHAPTER 9

EBONY

Shelley had come up with the most amazing idea. An online boutique. I could dress people around the globe! Any doubts I'd had were answered when Charlene had told me to 'Go for it'. I was still finding it strange talking to a newborn, but then again, my whole life had been one strange occurrence after another.

Feeling in a buoyant mood, I decided that even the moronic Henry wasn't going to spoil my vibe and I would be amazingly nice to him all afternoon. I needed to make an effort for Shelley and Theo's sake, and well, what was more annoying than someone you didn't like being nice to you? Also, it might stop Shelley calling a house meeting which would be extremely embarrassing.

I immediately made him a large mug of tea and walked up the stairs with it, having made sure there was nothing about the mug for him to find offensive. It was large, plain, and white, though no doubt he'd take it as a reference to his skin colour or say I was insinuating he was plain. The word fucktard came into my head, and I giggled. Being around Kim and the girls had rubbed off on me a little after all.

I knocked on the door of the room I could hear him moving around in. The smell of fresh paint hung in the air, making me cough slightly.

Henry opened the door.

"Yeah?"

"I brought you a mug of tea."

He eyed it suspiciously. "Why?"

"Because I just made hot drinks and thought you might like one." I smiled at him.

"What have you put in it?"

"One sugar and some milk, just how you said you took it." Oh, I was enjoying this a little too much.

"Oh-kay, well... thanks," he said, just as a vision of him tripping over a paint pot came to me.

"Can you stop that thing with your eyes. It's so weird," he complained, stepping backwards towards the paint pot.

I dashed to it, moving it out of his path and stood up smiling again.

"That's what my visions showed me was going to happen. You're very welcome for the rescue."

"It's nothing to do with bloody visions. I was only not looking where I was going because you went all weird again. Have you been to see a psychiatrist at all?"

I smiled brightly at him again.

"Well do enjoy your tea," I said. "I'll bring you another mug on the hour as I'm around for the rest of the afternoon."

I left the room highly amused at his confused expression.

Valentine's Day arrived, and I was on my way to the living room when my phone rang.

Lucy's voice echoed down the line. "Hey, Ebony. I have a hot date for you tonight. His name is Alexander and he's a vicar. Can you meet him at his parish at eight pm? He's going to take you to a dinner and dance."

"Sounds fantastic. Tell him I'll see him at eight." I ended the call.

Henry had just walked through the door. "You actually have a date tonight?"

"I do." I smiled.

"That's why you were nice to me yesterday. You're getting some. Now all becomes clear."

"Henry Marston. I have yet to have a date with the gentleman, and he's a vicar, so I am sure there will be none of me 'getting some' as you so succinctly put it. However, it will be lovely to get out for the evening and enjoy some hopefully pleasant company."

"A vicar? Sounds positively riotous."

I lowered my voice. "As for why I was nice to you yesterday... Shelley had spoken to me in the car and stated that if we continued to argue she was going to call a house meeting. Now I don't want that, so I figure why don't we just call a truce for however long I have to stay here to watch Charlene and you have to be here to decorate? I don't mind making you the occasional hot drink, if in turn you could stop calling my having visions weird."

"But it is weird."

"To you, yes. To me, well I've been having them for

years, so it's as natural to me as breathing. Now when they were excruciatingly painful, they drove me to vodka and my bed. It was more of a curse at times than a blessing, but at the moment I'm managing them fine which is putting me in a much better frame of mind. I want to enjoy myself while I can, Henry. Life's short. Hence tonight, I shall be waltzed around by a vicar at a dinner and dance, instead of being laid in bed with a migraine."

"Jax has had a couple of migraines at times. I know they suck. Yes, let's call a truce." He held his hand out and I took it in my own.

It was warm.

It was strong.

It made goose bumps go up my spine.

Casually, I moved my hand away. I could tell he was staring at me.

Then it happened again. My sight went dark until a vision came at me. Only this time I felt my arm be grasped, and myself be steered and lowered. I was aware of the sofa underneath my bottom.

As I came around from the vision, Henry was looking at me. This time with concern in his eyes.

"Are you all right, Ebony? I really think you should see a doctor. It could be some form of epilepsy."

"Is my handbag nearby?" I asked. He moved to the hallway and returned with it. A smirk tugged at my lips.

"What?"

"It's just you're all dark vested and muscly and carrying my pale-blue handbag. It's funny."

He quirked a brow and passed it to me.

Rummaging inside, I pulled out my phone.

"Hey, Lucy. Yeah, it's me. Cancel that date. I just had a vision of him with his lead chorister. Yeah, a man. I'm no one's beard. You might want to ask him his application questions again regarding his requirements. Yes, I can hold."

Lucy started clattering keyboard keys, and I heard her make a call on another line.

"Okay, now you are meeting a Jasper Monroe. He'll meet you at Hanif's at eight-thirty."

"Hanif's, eight-thirty, Jasper Monroe. What does he do?"

"He's a chef."

"A chef! Oh fantastic. Hopefully this will lead on to him cooking me dinner," I exclaimed. "Thanks, Lucy."

"You have another date already?" Henry said, looking annoyed.

"Yes, why?"

"No reason, other than thinking you probably should rest after your little fit thing."

"It's a vision, Henry." I sat up straight. "There's more in this world than you're aware of. Why not try opening your eyes a little more to the world around you? I have visions. Not fits, not delusions, not epilepsy. Visions. I saw your girlfriend dump you and I saw the bird poop on your head. I saw the paint pot whether I caused it or not. Now you can believe me or not, but if I warn you of something and you ignore me, you've no one but yourself to blame."

At that point Mary flounced into the room. "We've lots of visitors coming from tomorrow onwards, Ebony. I told them today was Valentine's and they could get lost. I've got a date, you know? The first since I was widowed. A date with a modern man. I can't wait. He's coming here at nine. It's been a century since my last date. If only I could get changed." She looked down at her cotton dress. Henry was turned towards me eye-rolling when she disappeared.

"A century. Likes to exaggerate does Mary, doesn't she? And why does she wear the same thing every day?"

"Open. Your. Eyes," I said to him again. Then I excused myself and left the room.

Dressing to impress, I put on a black fitted wrap dress and tongued my black hair into ringlets. A blue neon eyeliner made my eyes stand out, assisted by lashings of mascara. I added a bright red lip, and I was ready to go.

"You look lovely," Shelley said as she stood in the hallway rocking Charlene.

I can't wait until I can rock some Louboutins instead of frikkin bootees.

I tickled Charlene's chin. "See you later and I promise when you're older I will make sure your clothes are on point."

"Hey, what's wrong with what she has on now?" Shelley protested.

A 'my daddys' my hero' top and the apostrophe is in the wrong place. Please tell her it makes it look like I have lots of daddies.

"You might want to take a closer look at that top." I nodded towards it. I couldn't make Charlene grow any quicker, but I could help her mother's wardrobe choices.

"Oh shoot. I took her to the supermarket in that an

hour ago. Huh, I thought people were looking at me strangely."

———

I arrived at the restaurant just before eight-thirty and was greeted by Rav.

"Has Shelley forgiven me for the bodyguard stuff yet? What did she say to Theo?"

"You're safe. She told Theo she was pleased he cared enough to send a bodyguard around after her."

He breathed a sigh of relief.

"Then she held him up in the corner of the room with her webs and starved him of blood."

"What? He'll kill me."

"Ah, I was just messing with you, Rav." I laughed. "I'm sorry, I couldn't resist."

"Ebony!" Rav smirked. "I'm seeing a whole other side to you. So, do you have a reservation because it's the night of lurve."

"I do. I am meeting a Jasper Monroe."

Rav did a theatrical bow. "Please, my lady, this way."

I took a seat and ordered a glass of champagne. What the hell! It was Valentine's Day. I had a hot date due to arrive any minute and no painful visions. What more of an excuse did I need to celebrate?

Then fucktard walked in with a blonde. Of all the places to come, he had to bring his date here. He knew this was where my date was. Why didn't he change his own plans, or tell me he was coming here so I could have changed mine? I left the table and rushed to the ladies' bathroom. Hopefully by the time I returned my date would have arrived.

I poked my head out of the doorway. There was still no one at my table. I could see Henry looking around. He looked near where I was, so I quickly shot back into the bathroom.

Five minutes later, I did the same again, to find Henry walking towards the toilets. I still had no date at my table.

Hell's bells. I was going to have to hide again.

A loud knocking came on the outside of the door. I ignored it. It couldn't be him surely? Then I heard Rav's voice. "Ebony... Ebony, are you all right in there?"

Goddamn him.

I walked to the bathroom door and opened it. "Yes, I'm fine, thank you, Rav. I was just reapplying some make-up."

"Oh. It's just you'd been a while, so I wanted to make sure you hadn't fainted with one of your visions, or passed out drunk on vodka, or maybe got a stomach upset..."

"Like I said, I'm fine."

"Are you going to stay and eat because it doesn't look like your date's arriving and my bosses are saying they could re-book the table twenty times over tonight."

It was then I noticed that the door to the mens' was ajar, and it didn't take me too long to work out that my conversation was being listened in on.

"My date cancelled actually, Rav. He called me while I was in the bathroom. He's a top chef, and a well-known pop star—whose name I couldn't possibly divulge—offered him an obscene amount of money to cook for her and her date this evening. And he was willing to cancel this, for me. Of course, I said no, you mustn't. I am a modern woman and it's fine if the man needs to work. I am perfectly capable of eating a meal on my own. So, if you'll give me another minute to finish applying my mascara, I shall order my food. Thank you, Rav darling, though, for coming to check I was okay."

I closed the door and leaned back against the cold tiles and then I quickly moved away because God only knew what got coated down bathroom walls. I stared at myself in the mirror.

You can do this.

You are strong.

Another vision blew across me. This time of Henry getting his penis stuck in his zipper. I could have done without the visual, but it still made me feel better.

Looked like I wasn't the only one who was going to find dating painful tonight.

———

And stay and eat alone was exactly what I did. I ordered another glass of champagne, along with the pickle tray, a starter, and a main.

Henry walked back to his seat. Thankfully, his back was towards me. I watched the blonde's face. She kept smiling at him, but it didn't meet her eyes. She wasn't into him. Oh well, I guess as long as he 'got some' as he termed it, he wouldn't be too bothered. I sat ramrod straight and savoured every morsel of my delicious meal while all around me Valentine's Day things happened. A violinist came. He went to pass my table, but I stopped him and made him play. A woman walked around with red roses. She dropped one on my table and said it was from a secret admirer. I guessed Rav had given her the sad tale of my being the only singleton in Hanif's on Valentine's Day.

My meal eaten, I paid the bill and got up to leave.

Rav assisted me into my coat. "Thanks for the rose, Rav." I picked it up.

"It's not from me, Ebony," he said. "Oh, I've someone else wanting to pay their bill. Take care and I'll see you again soon."

I walked out of the restaurant and headed down towards the sea front. Maybe my mind had been playing tricks on me with the whole wedding business? I had just suffered from the spell blocking my visions. It must have been some after effect. Perhaps I just wasn't destined for love?

"Ebony. Wait up."

"Oh God," I muttered as I saw Henry rushing in my direction. I ducked into a side street to try to give him the slip. Right now, I didn't need his pity, and he needed to get back to his date, although I guessed that now he was on his way here I should warn him about his zipper.

"Are you trying to get attacked, going down dark alleys? Why are you trying to avoid me when I know damn well you saw me?"

"Henry, get back to your date. Oh and I need to warn you–"

Before I knew what was happening, Henry had pushed me back against the wall and crushed his lips to mine. A thousand thoughts hit me all at once.

· · ·

What the actual fuck?

Get off me.

What about your date?

Oh his body is crushing mine.

His chest is rock hard.

That's not all that's rock hard.

His lips are hot.

He's a great kisser. Etc etc...

Like my brain had left the building, I found myself returning the kiss hard. Henry's hands travelled down the V of the neck of my dress, trailing across a breast and teasing my nipple.

I could feel his hardness pressing against me and I had the most random thoughts. *I was living life right? Perhaps I should totally 'get some' outdoors, right now!*

"I want you, Henry. Now. Here."

His hands travelled to his zipper.

Oh God no. Was that what I'd seen?

"Henry. No," I yelled. "Don't."

He backed away like I'd slapped him. "I knew it. Decided I'm not good enough for you, have you? Forget it. I'm an idiot."

"No, no, let me explain."

"Save it," he said. "I hate bloody Valentine's Day. Now get a cab home before you're attacked, although it pains me to give a shit."

He walked away and all I could do was watch as he went out of sight.

CHAPTER 10

SHELLEY

It was Valentine's evening, and apart from having Charlie (asleep in her cot), and Mary being at the far end of the farmhouse enjoying chatting with her date (we'd made her a sitting room next to her bedroom for the occasion by moving a few pieces of furniture around), Theo and I found ourselves thankfully alone.

I'd bought us a bottle of a vintage O-neg to enjoy and we sat next to each other on the sofa curled up together.

"I don't remember the last time we had some peace and quiet. It's been very hectic lately, hasn't it?" I said to him.

"It really has. What with your turning, the were thing, and then Charlene's birth, it seems like forever since we got to cuddle on the sofa. We seem to permanently have interruptions."

I chewed on my bottom lip.

"What? Shelley. Tell me what's on your mind?"

"It's the B&B. Won't we have constant interruptions once that opens?"

He squeezed my hand. "Hopefully not too many.

Henry has everything in hand, and he has a builder friend who's going to help. The idea is to make the East side of the farmhouse the B&B. It will have its own sitting rooms, dining room etc, and then this side will be our home. I'm not offering evening meals and I'm not having a bar. I'll keep a vending machine for drinks and one for snacks and so it should cut down on guest interruptions. Plus, my mother will help. My vamp speed means cleaning is a doddle and doesn't take long. I'm excited about it. About seeing all the rooms of the farmhouse occupied. It's been empty for too long and it's such a beautiful building. While Henry is here, why don't you have a think about what you'd like doing with our half of the house?"

"Won't your mum object to any changes?"

He straightened. "It's not her house anymore. She's on a date tonight. She's moving on from her past; from her being a ghost widow. She needs to let go of her feelings for the past house too."

"Is it strange, your mum being on a date?"

"Not after all these years. I've seen so much that goes against normal since I was turned into a vampire. I look young, yet I'm 127. My mum looks only a few years older than me. Things aren't defined by the accepted societal norms. It's so long since I lost my father and I have only vague memories of him now. My mum must be the same. And she's now living in the year 2018 and wanting to embrace it."

"Do you think by moving on, she might actually disappear off to Heaven?"

Theo shrugged. "I really don't know. I guess that's a question for Frankie and his database of the supernaturals.

She's here because of her traumatic death. A happy relationship wouldn't change the fact I brutally murdered her in the farmhouse. She still gets pissed at me."

"Hmmmm. I can't believe I used to think my life was complicated if I had to choose between four different pairs of shoes before a night out."

"Do you miss that life?" he asked with an inflection in his tone.

I looked at my gorgeous husband and snuggled in closer.

"Not in the slightest. I have you and my daughter, and even with all the chaos that surrounds our lives, I couldn't be happier."

He lifted my hand and kissed the back of it. "Happy Valentine's Day, Mrs Theo Landry. I love you."

"Happy Valentine's Day, Mr Shelley Landry. I love you too." I gave him a peck on the lips.

"Like that is it?" Theo started to tickle me.

"Not fair. That's cheating. You know I can't..." I began to giggle.

"What's your name?"

"Shelley."

"What's your name?" The tickling was incessant, and I could hardly breathe.

"Mrs Theo... L-Landry. You cheating sod."

"Better." Theo winked. "Now as your reward I shall take you upstairs and ravish you."

We headed quietly up to the bedroom, not wanting to make what we were doing obvious, or wake Charlie, who was in the adjoining room, protected by as many wards as I could think up.

Theo slowly stripped me of all my clothing and then removed his own before joining me in the bed.

He moved above me and then we heard the noise.

"Whooooooo-oooooooooohhhhh-ooooooooooo."

We both stilled.

Theo stared at me. "What the hell is that noise?"

"Whooooooo-oooooooooohhhhh-ooooooooooo."

He leapt off the bed and began to put his trousers back on. "It sounds like my mum, like she's wailing. Don't you think it sounds like an unhappy ghost noise? Maybe she's realised how much she still misses my father after all."

"Whooooooo-oooooooooohhhhh-ooooooooooo. Ohhhhhhh yeeaaaaaaaaahhh."

Theo's alabaster face paled further.

I burst out laughing.

"I don't think she's missing him at all."

The next morning with Theo sound asleep, I walked into the kitchen to be met by a smiling translucent Mary. She hovered as if sitting at the kitchen table. Ebony sat at the side of her nursing a black coffee. She said good morning, but her expression didn't match her words.

"Good morning, Shelley. How was your Valentine's?" Mary beamed at me.

"Erm, nice. Thank you." How could I tell her it had been ruined by her own evening? There was no way me and Theo could get down and dirty after we realised what was going down in Mary's room and knowing it was possibly her date. Plus the wailing had gone on... and on...

and we had sensitive vampire ears. We would need therapy.

"I had the most fantastic date."

"Did you?"

"You have to hear all about it, like I have." Ebony grimaced. "Every single detail. Tell her, Mary, before you disappear. She's so full of it, her energy is wearing down."

"Let me get a coffee and then I'll come sit with you." I took a deep breath and hoped to God she didn't make me throw up.

"So. His name was Alistair, and he died in the 1990's. He went to a fancy-dress party as Madonna wearing a conical bra like she wore at the time and fell down the stairs because he couldn't see past them. He had a head injury. Luckily his parents changed him into a pair of nice navy-blue pyjamas before he died, and had taken his make-up off, or he'd have been stuck wearing his Madonna outfit, although to be fair I know anything goes these days and I'd have still given him a whirl. I'm very pleased to report he wasn't *Like a Virgin*."

I shared a look with Ebony that clearly said, 'Help'. She just looked at her drink. Cowbag.

"Anyhow, because he died in hospital, he's not tethered and can travel around Withernsea. However, he's furious and bitter about losing his life at the age of 27. Not least because someone had left a sausage roll on the stairs and that's what he slipped on. He was a vegetarian. Like he says, 'Meat is murder'. Apart from his meat... and two veg. He could accost me with his salami any time."

A bit of coffee sicked up into my throat.

"Anyway. It would appear that ghosts can fuel each

other up a little because even though we were at it all night, we never got tired! I learned so much! In my day you had to be very demure and let the man take charge. Well, let me tell you. I sucked on that stick like it was a Sherbet Dib Dab, and his tongue... he went down—"

"Stairs. Downstairs. Got it. Don't need to hear any more of the actual who did what. You had a nice date. That's all I need to hear. A. Nice. Date."

Mary rolled her eyes. "I had a very nice date." She paused for a beat. "And fourteen orgasms."

"Mary!"

She chuckled. "That's not all."

"I don't think my ears can take any more, Mary."

"Because we 'joined', somehow when I'm with him, he can take me out of the house."

I sat up straighter.

"He can?"

"Yes, so we're off out for the day. After a century I'm getting out of here. Don't wait up." And with that she disappeared.

It took me a moment to find my voice again.

"I'm putting brandy in my coffee even though it's five past nine in the morning and you will not judge me."

Ebony pushed her mug forward. "Let's do it."

I put a tot in each drink and topped them up with a little more water.

"Cheers."

"What's up with you this morning?" I asked her.

Ebony sighed. "My date didn't show last night. I ate in a packed restaurant on Valentine's Day all by myself."

I reached across for her hand. "Oh, Ebony. I'm sorry. If

it's any consolation, we spent all night listening to Mary wailing."

"Yes, me too. Three am until five am, when I eventually resorted to cutting up a pair of bed socks and stuffing the material in my ears."

"I have vampire hearing."

"You win."

"Theo has vampire hearing *and* it's his mother."

"Oh my goodness. Poor Theo. Oh well, at least she can leave the house now. As long as she stays with this Alistair, the sex noises can take place elsewhere."

The sound of a van came up the drive, and I looked out of the kitchen window. "Henry's here. Theo was telling me all the plans for the B&B last night. I'm actually coming around to the idea now."

"Oh, that's great."

"Yeah, and Theo said I could decorate our side of the house however I wanted, so there'll be plenty of work for Henry. I'm going to ask him if he has any paint samples or charts."

"Excellent."

"Ebony, you said excellent as if it compared to you being hung, drawn, and quartered. Do you really dislike him that much?"

We were interrupted by the door opening.

"In here, Henry," I shouted.

He put his head through the door. "Morning, Shelley." I noted he made a point to completely leave Ebony out of his greeting. She stared at the table.

"Morning, Henry. Would you like a drink?"

"No, I'm fine actually. I've brought a flask today and a

couple of bottles of water. Just going to crack on." With that he started up the stairs.

"Has something else happened?" I folded my arms across my chest as I stared at Ebony.

She pushed her mug forward again. "This time I'll take it without the coffee."

I refused to give Ebony any more alcohol as my first visitors were due to arrive within the hour.

She wouldn't go into detail, just stating she'd seen Henry while out last night and they'd got into an argument. I really needed to do something, but right now it was time to get myself and Charlene ready for her visitors.

"Are you sure you feel okay enough to be around the visitors?" I asked her.

"Absolutely." This time Ebony genuinely smiled. "It's an absolute honour to be around Charlie."

"Hey, you're calling her Charlie too. Thank you. Everyone else is still calling her Charlene. I like it shortened. It sounds fun. What made you change your mind?"

"I don't think Charlie minds whichever she's called."

"Yeah true. It's not like she understands what's happening, is it? She has so much of the world to learn about."

"Er, yeah. You know babies. Taking in everything around them."

———

Darius was the first visitor to the house, coming in an official capacity as Alpha of the Withernsea Pack, rather than as my best friend's husband. It was strange to see him dressed in his ceremonial robes.

He gave me a hug which engulfed me. He was a rugged beast and had the warmest personality. My friend had done very well for herself. Behind him stood his sister Alyssa. It was only a week ago that I'd watched as she tore out the throats of two rogue weres, yet here she stood looking every inch the stroppy teenager. Appearances could definitely be deceptive. I hugged Alyssa hard, as not only had she done the bravest of things, but she'd now reminded me that no matter what my guests of the morning looked like, I wasn't to trust the ones I didn't know.

"Alyssa, I shall allow you to hold the baby first." Darius' voice boomed around the living room. He sounded like Thor.

She pulled a face. "You will allow me? Jesus." She turned to me. "He talks like this all the time you know now? Bloody alpha. Kim digs it for her own reasons, but all I hear is too much testosterone sloshing around." She stood up, and I handed her the baby. "You are so cool. There aren't enough girlies around here. You can be my new bestie."

Darius passed me a gift. "This is an official gift from the Pack."

I unwrapped the gift to find a photo frame. Behind the frame was a large tooth. "That is a fang from the first Alpha of the Withernsea Pack. It is there in order for us to declare that we offer our help to Charlene whenever she shall need it. The fang is to show that we would savage anyone who would wish harm on her or her kingdom. And of course while we wait for her to take over, you know we pledge the same to you as our current Queen."

"Thank you, Darius. Charlene is extremely fortunate to

have such a loving tribe behind her." And yes, I was currently ruler of Withernsea, and I'd not got a fang. But then again there wasn't a prophecy about me being the most badass ruler ever either. My daughter was foretold to be quite something. Hard to imagine while she cooed, pulled grimaces, and filled her nappy.

But I was happy for her to go to reins before reign. I was going to enjoy every bit of having my baby and watching her grow up, even if that did mean I had to entertain half of Withernsea in between.

CHAPTER 11

SHELLEY

"Damn. Mary's gone out and I forgot to ask her who else is visiting."

Ebony looked up at me from her seat on the sofa. She put the fashion magazine she'd been reading down on her knees. "I know she said someone at one pm and someone at three pm. She spaced them out." She wrinkled her nose. "Oh, I remember. The pixies are coming, then it's someone from the sea."

"Oh God. Please tell me I'm not getting another bucket of fish on my head."

"You should be safe. It'll be Charlie they might want to pour sea water on."

"They can go whistle."

She smirked.

"Great. Bloody Tristan's coming first. Charlie, your next visitor is an arsehole."

I'd first met Tristan, the leader of the pixies, at a speed dating event. Charming he was not. His ego was larger than his body. Luckily, I'd never got as far as Lucy had. Poor

Lucy had suffered an unfortunate sexual encounter with him pre-Frankie where she discovered that although he was well endowed for a pixie, for her she hadn't been able to... well, feel it. Anyway, the situation had been smoothed over. I just had to hold my temper, think of being patient, and hopefully he wouldn't stay long.

I figured I'd better greet him at the door myself given what Brishon had been like when he'd visited. On swinging the door ajar, I discovered that not only was Tristan on my doorstep, but he'd brought six other pixies with him. He was wearing a charcoal grey suit. Tristan was a good-looking guy but unfortunately his personality made him ugly.

"Hello, Shelley. I am here to visit your daughter." He was straight and to the point as always.

"Come in, Tristan, and... your friends too of course."

"They are my entourage, not my friends."

Here we go. *Bite your tongue, Shelley. Even if it bleeds.*

I escorted them through to the living room. Ebony nodded that everything was okay and went off to make Tristan a drink. Apparently, his entourage were forbidden from drinking until after he'd finished his own.

Tristan peered over the side of Charlie's crib.

"Robust bones. Shame it's a girl, but if the prophecy says she's the one, then she's the one."

One. Two. Three. Four. Five... breathe, Shelley, breathe. Do not put a spell on him!

Charlie remained asleep. Ebony returned. "Your Coke and a straw as requested."

"Well don't give it to me, girl. Give it to him." He pointed to one of his crew. "What are you waiting for, Bryan? Christmas?" The pixie leapt forward for the glass and held it to Tristan's mouth while he took a drink.

"Mikkel. Come forward with the gift now please. Place it in front of the crib."

Mikkel did as asked.

Tristan cleared his throat.

"Charlene Kimberly Landry. I, Tristan, Leader of the Withernsea Pixies, hereby declare our support to you where it be needed. In war or," he coughed, "in matters of love."

Was he seriously suggesting he'd shag my daughter if she needed it? Please mean he'd help her find a suitor.

He turned to me. "If she needs to further the line, I would be honoured."

Nope, he meant shag her.

"Thank you for your kind offer, Tristan. As I stated to Duke Brishon yesterday, Charlie will choose her own suitor when able."

"Duke Brishon? What was that toerag proposing? He's a billion years old."

"Not him, his son Lord Drake," Ebony informed him. She obviously had a death wish.

"Lord Drake?" Tristan's face went puce. "And what did you say to this?" He glared at me. "Because if he gets first refusal, I shall take you to court for diversity. The little people shall not be ignored." He swung his arm in the air.

"Tristan. I told Duke Brishon the same as I am telling you. Charlie will choose her *own* suitor. And speaking of diversity, no one knows if her intended is even male, or supernatural for that matter."

"Do you know about my legendary manhood? She would be very satisfied. What would she do with a woman?"

I wasn't getting into this.

"Were you not in the middle of your speech?"

He paused. "Oh yes." He turned back to the crib.

"From the date of your birth until the date of my death, I give you the freedom of the realm of the pixies." He opened the box at his feet and removed a key and handed it to me.

"I never knew you had a realm, Tristan. Thank you. On behalf of Charlene, I thank you for your generous offering."

"It's the key to Withernsea Waffles on the seafront."

"Sorry?"

"Withernsea Waffles. We keep it on the down low, but that is our kingdom. It is not confined to waffles of course, but sugared doughnuts and burgers do not begin with a w."

"You own the unit on the seafront?"

"I am pleased to say I do. Should you ever want a coffee and a sugared doughnut please visit."

"That's very kind, Tristan."

"It'll be £2.99 to you, usual price. Of course Charlene can have whatever she wishes for free, although obviously it's a business not a charity so don't go mad. A moment on the lips, hey Charlene? Can't fulfil the prophesy if you're a heifer who can hardly move."

"I'm just going to change Charlene's nappy and then I'd be very honoured if you would hold her."

"Yes, that would be most fitting. As Pixie Leader, I need to have held the newborn."

I left the room with Charlie who didn't need her nappy changing at all, but I didn't know how to clear up dead pixie body and anyway what if he then haunted the place like Mary and I was stuck with him forever? I shuddered. Charlene just made baby gurgling noises. "Well you're no help, little lady today." Then I had a thought. "Though you could be..."

On my return I passed the baby to Tristan and he sat awkwardly on the sofa.

There were footsteps on the stairs and then Henry popped his head around. "I've run out of white emulsion. Thought I'd have enough to finish this room, but it needs an extra coat." He looked at everyone. "Oh, hello. What's going on here? I saw you guys in the panto at Christmas, didn't I?"

Tristan went puce in the face again. "It is dwarves who do panto. I am the leader of the pixies. How very dare you." He looked at my daughter as if deciding where he could put her while he launched at Henry.

My daughter made a puce face of her own and then an almighty godawful smell came from her.

I'm sorry, Charlie. Please forgive me, but... thank you. I promise I'll give you a bath and a baby massage after.

I lifted my daughter from his lap. "Oh no. I forgot to put her a new nappy on. Seriously, I have complete baby brain. I've lost my mind." I whipped her away from Tristan who looked down to see he was covered in a yellowy-green foul-smelling shit sludge.

"Aaarrrrrrgggghhhh. Get it off me. Get it off me." He launched off the sofa, shaking at his clothes. Then he looked at Henry, who unfortunately had started to laugh.

Tristan launched, knocking Henry to the floor and coating him in my daughter's poop.

"Could you please deal with your leader?" I asked Bryan and the others. "And remove him from my home." I turned to Tristan on the floor. "Tristan, I thank you for your gift but if you could kindly leave now, I have further guests due shortly."

I looked at Ebony who was shrieking with laughter at the shit-wrestling happening right in front of her. She looked at my daughter.

"Oh, Charlie. I adore you. A class act."

"I'm going to get her cleaned up. Could you please tell Henry he can use the shower again when Tristan finally leaves?"

"Sure thing," Ebony said, then she sat back on the sofa. Didn't look like she was in any rush for the fun to end.

On my way out, Bryan pulled on my arm. "I apologise on behalf of my people." He lowered his voice. "And also, I do indeed star in panto every Christmas, but don't tell Tristan I moonlight. Free entry for your family anytime."

I thanked him and left the room.

CHAPTER 12

EBONY

I really tried my hardest not to laugh, but a pixie was on the floor wrestling with a six-foot-something man mountain, and I'd have to say things were pretty much even. Tristan was small but mighty, which I guess was a prerequisite for the leader. Every time they rolled around, more of Charlene's poop transferred itself to Henry. She'd not communicated a word to me this morning, but she'd certainly communicated her opinion of Tristan.

The rest of the pixies lifted Tristan away from Henry. Stepping back, Tristan put his head back and held his nose high in the air. "Thank you for the drink, Ebony. I shall be on my way."

My vision went dark, and I saw something that in a strange way made a lot of sense. A vision about his future. It wasn't for a while yet as the love of his life looked different in my vision to how she did now, but she was coming.

Tristan had paused in front of me. "Ebony, what did you see?"

I smiled at him. "Tristan, it's not imminent, but your 'one' is coming. You will be very happy together. She's lovely."

Despite the fact he was coated in poop, he beamed at me and dropped to a bow.

"Ebony, you have made my day. Thank you, kind lady." He looked at the others. "We shall show ourselves out."

They left, leaving me in the room with Henry who stood glowering.

"If you want to get showered, I'll run your clothes through the machine."

I could tell by his expression he didn't want me anywhere near him. However, he stank to high heaven, so he had no choice but to follow me up the stairs. "You can use the guest bathroom that I use. Oh, and I use unperfumed shower gel, so you won't smell girly." I pushed open the door and he followed me in. I didn't realise how small the bathroom was until we were sharing the same space.

"Okay, thanks. You can go now," he dismissed me.

I glared at him. "Karma came to you. You deal shit out; you get it back." I made sure to emphasise the word 'shit' that he was so fond of.

What I didn't expect was for him to flick his t-shirt at me, coating me in Charlie's finest.

"Yuck. You did not just do that." I pulled a face and shivered.

Then without thinking, I stripped my top straight off. It was one thing to have to endure the sight and smell on someone else. Quite another for it to be on me and directly under my nose.

I realised Henry was staring at me.

"I'm going in the shower first now. You'll have to wait," I told him and I drew back the curtain, stepped into the bath, then closed the curtain in his face. I threw the rest of my clothes over the top of the curtain and then noted I'd not got myself a towel. Fuck, I was stuck naked in the bath. Sighing I flipped the shower on. Then the curtain moved slightly, and a naked Henry got in at the side of me.

My jaw hit the floor.

"Henry, get out. You can't be in this shower with me. That's totally an invasion of my personal space to a degree so high I can't even count that far."

"Move over, you don't even have any shit on you. It was only a tiny bit on your top. I got covered in it."

"How do you know it didn't seep through? It was very watery."

"Move." He went to move me but accidentally grabbed my breast.

There we stood. Him frozen in mortification while he awkwardly remained standing there with my breast in his hand. Then he dropped it and turned ready to get out of the shower. He looked back at me.

"I'm sorry. You just make me feel lots of confusing feelings all at once. I don't know whether to hate you or kiss you."

I sighed. "So kiss me, you idiot."

"But last night..."

"Last night I got a vision of you getting your penis stuck in your zipper. I was trying to warn you."

His eyes searched mine. "You mean, you weren't turning me down?"

"No. I was totally going to embrace some alfresco sex and live a little."

He groaned. "I had blue balls for no reason."

"Well, if I hadn't intervened, you'd have had a black and blue todger."

He smirked. "Ebony, for fuck's sake, call it my cock."

I sighed and reached out, stroking him.

"I'd like your cock inside my pussy please, Henry."

A serious groan escaped his mouth. "Jesus, I came already. Tell me more."

"Yeah, when you're clean." I handed him a sponge and the shower gel.

As soon as that hot as hell body was clean, I found myself backed against the tiled wall, the cold hitting my skin and making my nipples harden further. They were soon warmed by Henry's mouth as one by one he sucked on them.

His fingers slid between my thighs, teasing at my core until the pressure built and I exploded over his digits. My breath came in short gasps. I reached for him again and stroked his length in my hand. Gently, I ran my manicured nails up and down him.

"I can't wait any longer."

He pushed inside me, the feeling exquisite, and my back continued to be pushed against the wall as he kissed me fervently. Our tongues tangled until we had to part to be able to catch our breath. With a final thrust, he took us both over the edge, and then we stood resting against the wall, his forehead against mine as we tried to get our breathing back under control, and in my case, try to stop my legs from bowing out beneath me.

"That was incredible," he whispered in my ear.

"EBONYYYYYY. Where are you? The next visitors are here."

"Oh shoot," I yelled. Shelley needs me. I'd better get dressed and towel my hair quickly. I looked at him. "Henry, I still need to wash your clothes."

Henry shook his head. "I always have spare overalls with me. You get ready and I'll do the same."

I towelled off my hair and body, quickly dressed, and headed downstairs back to the living room.

Charlie was in the hands of a tall man with long red hair. He wore green-blue satin trousers that looked like fish scales, and no shirt. My whole opinion of his outfit must have shone through on my face.

"This is Kai. He is the leader of the Mermen," Shelley introduced me. "His merman legs turn into these funky trousers. Groovy aren't they?" Shelley's face was sending clear signals that this was not the time for me to dish out fashion advice.

He's fucking hot, isn't he, Auntie Ebony? And his hands are so smooth and warm.

Completely inappropriate baby talk, Charlene Landry.

Charlie let out an audible sigh.

"Oh listen to that. You have the magic touch. She looks very contented in your arms."

"I'll say," I added.

Kai smiled a huge beam at me and then turned to Shelley, nodding in my direction. "It is very pleasing that your subject came to me damp."

"Excuse me?" *How did he know my panties were a little wet from thinking about what I'd just done with Henry?*

"Your skin. It is damp, yes, and your hair?"

"Ohhh. Yes."

"It is custom… not for the Queen." he nodded towards Shelley. "But for others to present themselves wet or damp to me as leader of the Mermen. It is very polite."

When I've grown up I'll present myself to him w—

"Charlie!" I didn't realise I'd shouted out loud.

Shelley looked at me worriedly. "Is she in danger?"

Kai looked disgusted. Oh God, I was causing chaos.

I held a hand to my chest. "Sorry, I thought she might have broken wind and she had an accident on a guest earlier. My apologies, Sir, for alarming you, and you too, Queen Shelley." If he thought I was a subject, I'd better go the whole hog.

"She's fine and has a nappy on anyway," Shelley said, but Kai passed her back to Shelley all the same.

Now look what you did.

You caused it!

"If you shall hold Charlene for me, I will make my speech and present my gift."

Kai bowed at Shelley and Charlene's feet. I didn't mind because from here I could see his tight butt in those strange pants. I shook my head. What was wrong with me? Had Henry made me a sex-crazed monster?

"Charlene Kimberly Landry. It is the honour of myself and the mermen of Withernsea to serve you and protect you." He opened the jewelled box at his feet and held it open to Shelley. "Inside here is a golden bejewelled whistle. Should you or Charlene need me, or my men, you blow on this whistle, and we shall be here as fast as our fins and land legs can carry us." He stood again.

"Kai. This is a truly wonderful gift, and your speech was beautiful. We also will help you if needed in any way that we can."

Kai bowed and then leaning over kissed the top of Charlie's forehead.

I just fainted, Auntie Ebony. Fan me.

"I shall be on my way. Until we meet again, ladies."

I escorted him to the door where he bid me farewell.

When I turned Henry was behind me.

"I saw you checking out his butt."

I smiled. "It's not as nice as yours."

"Come out with me tonight, Ebs."

He called me Ebs!

"I'm quite a good cook. How about you come to mine, and I'll make us dinner? It's been ages since I entertained. Usually, a vision comes and I end up in bed with a migraine, cutting the evening short."

"I foresee you'll end up in bed again, but not with a migraine."

"Ahem."

We both shot around to face Shelley.

"Well, well. Looks like we don't need a house meeting any more, Charlie. Unless they both have damp hair because they had a nasty water fight? Hmmmm. No, I don't think so either."

"Is the... is the baby... talking to you?" I asked.

Shelley rolled her eyes. "Ebony, honestly. Don't be silly. I think it's a good idea you get out tonight. You need a break from all these visitors and being cooped up in here, it's addling your brain."

As if a baby can talk, Auntie Ebs. Honestly!

Be quiet you or I'll put that nursery rhyme CD on repeat in your room.

I noticed both Henry and Shelley were staring at me. "Hot drink anyone?" I said and dashed to the kitchen.

CHAPTER 13

SHELLEY

I put Charlie in her crib, walked into the bathroom and turned on the tap. I needed some me-time. In one morning I'd endured a wailing orgasmic ghost, a miserable seer, an asshole pixie, as well as also being visited by weres and a merman. Then I found out that while I wasn't getting any, everyone else seemed to be. It was making me extra grumpy, so a nice soak in the tub it was.

A knock came to the outside door, and huffing, I opened it to find Ebony on the other side.

"There's a merman at the door. He says Kai forgot something."

"Couldn't he just give it to you?"

"Apparently not."

I did my best not to stomp downstairs, although it was difficult, and I stood in the doorway looking at the man in front of me. Long blonde hair was flicked off his face. The guy looked like a merman Fabio.

He stood with a box in his hand.

"My leader forgot to bestow upon you one of his gifts,"

he said. Then he promptly proceeded to throw sea water at me again.

"Good day, Queen," he added, walking away with the box as I spluttered a piece of seaweed out of my mouth.

I held a finger up to Ebony, who took my cue not to say a damn word. Instead, she passed me a hand towel from the kitchen. I quickly ran it over my face and hair.

"My bath awaits. Unless Charlie disturbs, I shall be unavailable. Even if Withernsea itself is in peril. I shall Not. Be. Disturbed."

"Got it. Go chill," Ebony said.

I nodded at her and made my way back upstairs.

An hour later I felt different again. The warm water had soothed my tense muscles. I no longer smelled of the sea, and I'd done a quick defuzz everywhere and covered myself in a nicely scented body lotion.

Slipping between the sheets next to my still sleeping husband I decided I'd laze around for a while.

I woke to find Theo looking down at me. Charlie in his lap.

"I've fed her one of your expressed bottles."

"You didn't need to do that. It's not like I need much sleep."

"What were you doing in bed? Couldn't resist me?"

"It's been a wearing day with visitors."

"I'm sorry you're left to deal with this alone. Why not get the visitors to come at night so I can help you?"

"Yeah, I might sometimes, but right now, I'm glad it's just us."

"And Ebony, and my mother, and possibly Henry if he's still here."

I shook my head. "Ebony and Henry are on a date at her house. Your mother is on a date at her new boyfriend's. She said for us to not wait up."

Theo's eyes widened. "She was able to leave the house?"

Daughter or not, Charlie was back in that crib by the time I uttered the word, "Yes."

"We have the house to ourselves. Oh thank the Lord. It's time to make my good wife scream the house down."

"Well not too loudly cos we might wake the baby," I said, but Theo's hearing was already muffled by his head being halfway down the bedsheets.

CHAPTER 14

Well, my mind might be confused but my body seemed to be handling things.

I'd thought Ebony was gorgeous the first time I'd set eyes on her in my sister's coffee shop a couple of years ago. However just as I'd been introduced to her, her face had gone grey and her eyeballs had rolled showing the whites. I'd quickly lifted up my mobile phone, only for Jax to hold my arm, telling me that Ebony did this quite often and said it was due to visions.

When she'd come to a few minutes later, Ebony had mumbled something about seeing a vision of a vampire wanting a date. Well, that was that. The woman was beautiful but entirely cuckoo.

I'd been dating Callie. Lust had turned into comfortableness. I'd said I loved her because I thought I did, and also, she said it to me and sulked if I didn't say it back. Things had been good, until they weren't. Now I knew why. Once she'd dumped me, I'd decided I'd have a bit of time 'single and ready to mingle' and 'playing the field'.

Any number of clichés about getting my dick wet, I would embrace them all.

But the gorgeous but bloody barmy Ebony was in my life again. I'd tried, and now obviously failed, to resist her. A date was good. A date at her house meant getting to know her and checking out what she was getting at, telling me to open my eyes. While I spent more time with her alone, I'd be able to assess just how bonkers she was and whether it was worth a little madness in my life to have that fine body riding me for hours. I got hard just thinking about it.

Calling in at the supermarket on my way to her house, I bought a bottle of an expensive wine as I doubted Ebony would be impressed by a bottle from the bargain bucket. Then I drove the short ten-minute drive from my house to hers.

She opened the door looking so damn hot in a tight red dress.

"Come in, the food's almost ready. I just need to do your steak."

"Thank you." As she walked ahead, I checked out my appearance in her hallway mirror before following her.

"You look gorgeous," I said, bending down and giving her a kiss on the cheek.

"Thank you. You scrub up well too."

I handed the bottle of wine over. "It's a good one. I think."

That earned me a look. "Henry, you will get to know hopefully over the course of the evening that I am a normal human being, well, apart from my visions. I do enjoy a glass of champagne, but I can also appreciate a half of cider. I've lived in Withernsea a long time now."

Over dinner she spoke about her family back in London. I knew from Jax that Ebony had lost her mum in a house fire. I told her about growing up as the older brother of a tiny tearaway called Jax. Conversation flowed easily until before I knew it she was offering me a coffee, the meal was over and it was a quarter to eleven at night. She'd not had a vision at all. Maybe they were an attention seeking kind of thing and because she had my attention, she'd not felt the need to 'perform'?

We sat on the sofa and clutching my coffee I tried to bring the conversation around to us ending up shagging in her bathroom.

"What was all that about earlier, right, with that short guy? What was he doing at the house anyway? If you don't mind me pointing out, Shelley lets some strange people in the house. That last one didn't have a shirt on and looked like he'd poofed out of the 1970's!"

Ebony sighed and bit on her bottom lip. "Henry, I'm going to tell you something and I want you to hear me out. Not go off about me being crazy, just listen. Then we'll say no more about what I've told you and you can do your own research into it."

Oh dear, was Ebony about to come out with something cuckoo and ruin the good vibe we had going on?

"I can already see by your face that you still think I'm a sandwich short of a picnic. I can't blame you. If it were the other way around, I'd already be out of the door." She grabbed hold of my hand. "Just hear me out, okay? Then if you want, you can leave."

As her hand held mine the strangest sensation travelled over my wrist, up my arm, and across my shoulder, my neck, until an electrical style jolt hit my brain. My vision went black and then pictures flashed over my mind. Theo with fangs. Shelley with blue threads coming out of her fingers holding what looked like Satan up in the air. Darius as a werewolf. I dropped her hand and leaped back away from her.

"What was that? What the fuck just happened?"

Ebony sat there staring at her hand. "What did happen? I, I felt a spark come from my hand and then your eyes rolled and you went pale. Did you... did you see things?"

"Is it some kind of virus? One that gives hallucinations? I saw Theo with fangs. Other weird shit." I sprang off the sofa and moved towards the door. "Did you drug me? Did you put something in my food?"

"You experienced what I do." Ebony now had tears falling down her face. "You had some kind of vision. Please, please, let me tell you everything and then you can think I'm crazy, drugged you, and you never have to see me again. I'll tell Shelley I can't help her anymore, but please, just hear me out, Henry."

Her gaze was pleading, and she looked so desperate that I found myself walking back to the sofa.

She asked me to wait and came back with another bottle, this time vodka. "You might need something stronger than the coffee."

"I already had my limit this evening. I'm driving."

She looked up at me. "You can stay. I have a spare room if you prefer. Or I can phone for a taxi to take you home."

I sighed. "Go on then, pour me a drink."

Ebony swallowed. "I've been having visions since I was young. They got stronger after my mother passed. She was also a seer like me. I get warning visions but sometimes they aren't much use to people, only a snippet. I predicted that Shelley would end up with Theo; that Kim would marry Darius.

"Theo is a vampire. He's 127 years old. Shelley was turned just before Charlie's birth. She's also part witch and part wyvern. Frankie Love, who you probably know, has an app you can sign up to that teaches you all about the supernaturals of Withernsea. There are a lot of us. Your sister, Jax, has no idea of what we are at this moment in time, although things change."

I took a drink of my vodka. "You realise this sounds absolutely cray-cray, right, and by all accounts I should be running the hell out of here and phoning you a psychiatrist?"

"Tristan who you fought today is the leader of the pixies of Withernsea. Darius visited as the leader of the Withernsea pack. Kai with the nice bottom is the leader of the mermen."

I snorted.

"Charlene will rule all of Withernsea when she's older. The prophecy states she'll save Withernsea from destruction and no one will have ever seen anyone like her. That's why they are all visiting. They are offering their servitude. I'm staying because if I get a vision warning of Charlie being in danger from any of them, I can pass it straight on and warn Shelley and Theo. I can help keep her safe."

Just as I was about to tell her I was out of here, her words from earlier whispered into my mind. *Open your eyes.*

I thought about the fact that Theo slept in the daytime

and came out at night. That he talked about poor circulation if you touched him because he was cold.

Shelley telling me that I could help myself to anything in the fridge, except her tomato juice, because it was a rare variety and expensive.

The weird Mary who was always here one minute and not the next.

I looked across at Ebony. "Who's Mary, Ebony?"

She swallowed. "Mary is Theo's mother. She's a ghost who up until today was tethered to the house. Theo drained her when he was first turned into a vampire. That's why you only see her occasionally. She runs out of energy and goes translucent or disappears completely."

"Right."

"I know it's a lot to take in and seems crazy. Right now, you think you're dreaming right, or you need a psychiatrist? I know because at one time I was you."

This statement made me focus on her, take note of her words.

"Once I didn't have visions and then I did, and my mum told me this was all real and I wasn't going insane. Then the visions showed me mystical beings that had only ever been in story books, and I said 'No, Mama. You need to get me to a doctor because I'm ill. The children at school are calling me crazy'. But you know." A tear slid down her face. "You get used to pretending people's hurtful talk doesn't harm you after a while. You get used to the name calling and the fact everyone thinks you should be out of the community and into an asylum."

I wiped the tears from her eyes.

"Why haven't you run yet, Henry?"

"I don't know," I said honestly, and then I leaned over and kissed her because if I was going mad I might as well enjoy the ride.

The next morning I awoke in Ebony's bed. I turned towards her. She was still asleep, looking peaceful and angelic, her dark hair splayed out across the pillow.

The memories of everything she'd told me and what I'd seen in that weird hallucination rushed back. I couldn't make sense of any of it, but I owed it to Ebony to go back to the farm with her this morning and find out the truth.

I got out of bed, deciding for once I'd make Ebony a hot drink. As I left the room, I found I was shaking my head. Was I really believing this was real? Maybe I was going cray-cray too?

CHAPTER 15

EBONY

I woke up, the ache between my legs reminding me of the glorious early hours of the morning where we'd not been able to get enough of each other. Then I turned over and saw the space next to me. I sat up and noted there were none of his clothes around my bedroom. A huge thumping sadness beat against my chest as I registered the fact he'd gone. Then I heard a noise downstairs. The clattering was followed by an "Oh shit," from a familiar voice, and I let out a large exhale as both relief and joy flooded my body that he was still here. Footsteps padded up the stairs and Henry walked in holding two steaming mugs.

"One coffee for the lady," he said putting my mug at the side of my bed.

He walked back around to 'his' side and placed his mug on the bedside table there before flopping back onto the bed. "And a nice cuppa for me."

"I thought you'd left," I told him honestly. "When I saw the clothes gone."

His mouth dropped open slightly as he looked around the room. "Oh God, I'm sorry. I just wanted to be dressed as I didn't know if you had a maid coming in or anything. I didn't want you to be sued or to cause heart failure to anyone."

"A maid! Oh, Henry, what are you going to come out with next? Do you want to have sex against a tree and call me Lady Chatterley?"

"Not only posh folks have maids. My mum hates cleaning. She has a maid service come round once a week."

"Fair enough. It's a shame you're dressed though." I bit my lip.

"You are aware clothes come off right? Let me show you."

And he did.

Henry said he'd drive us both across to the farmhouse.

After showering and dressing, I heard him honking the van horn and realised it was almost nine am. Locking the door behind me, I ran down the path and jumped into the passenger seat of the van. The front footwell was full of discarded crisp packets and chocolate wrappers, plus empty pop bottles.

"Sorry about the mess."

"You're a filthy pig," I told him.

"You weren't complaining last night... or this morning." He chuckled.

My phone rang and I answered it. Kim started speaking.

"Ebs, babe. I got you another date, and yes, I am here before nine am. Can you have a vision to see what I'm coming down with because it's not normal. I actually thought I'd better be here to open up as Lucy can't get here until ten am. I'm sick, Ebs. Sick."

"You're not sick. Well, I've not had any such visions about you anyway. Perhaps you are either growing up, or you're scared of what Shelley would say if she found out the place wasn't open on time."

"I suppose. Shelley really is bloody terrifying when she gets a mood on. Anyway, you owe me big time. I have got you a date with..." She made a drumroll noise. "Dmitri Rosario from Withernsea AFC. You're welcome."

"Actually, Kim, I was going to ring to tell you." I looked across at Henry, who was glaring out of the front windscreen. His knuckles were clenched around the steering wheel so tightly I was surprised it hadn't come off in his hand. "I'm seeing someone. It's early days, but you know me. I don't want to see anyone else at the same time. Can you cancel my membership?"

Henry looked at me and grinned, his shoulders coming back down from around his ears.

"But it's Dmitri Rosario."

"I don't care if it's Henry Cavill." I thought about it. "No, actually, scratch that. If you get Henry Cavill I'll go." A hand came over and nipped my arm several times lightly.

"Ouch."

"No Henry's other than me," he said.

The phone went silent on the other end. "Ebs, are you getting it on with Henry Marston? As in Jax's brother?"

"You breathe a word, and I will see if I can deliberately invoke a vision where you no longer orgasm."

"But... but..."

"No one. Not right now. He needs to tell Jax himself, not have it blurted out from you."

"Shit. I never thought of that," Henry mumbled at the side of me.

"Oh, okay. But feed me some gossip to keep me going. Anything. Is he good in bed?"

I giggled. "Kim, Henry has the most divine cock." Then I ended the call.

The van swerved on the word cock. "Jesus, woman. Are you trying to kill us? You can't dirty talk the word cock at the side of me like that when I'm driving."

I arched a brow at him. "Your magnificent dick needs to rub against my core. To enter my pussy and have me begging for you to ride me hard. Oh... so... hard."

Henry veered the van off down the next country lane. "We're going to be late for work now, but hopefully not arrested for public sex. Get in the back of my van. Thank God, I always carry plenty of bedsheets."

I called Shelley to apologise for being late, saying Henry had suffered a flat tyre. Shelley told me I was a hopeless liar and that it was okay because she was happy for me.

As we walked through the door Theo was there.

"Morning," he said yawning.

"Theo. Shouldn't you be in bed?" I queried.

"Yes, I absolutely should, and I'm off in a minute, but

I've developed the start of your new fashion website and I was too excited to show you, to go to sleep."

"And this is the morning I choose to be late. I'm sorry, Theo." Turning, I touched Henry's arm. "I'll see you later. Let's go, Theo. I can't wait."

"Just a second," Henry said. "Shelley, do you have a minute?"

Shelley came out into the hallway. "Yeah?"

"Ebony was pointing some things out to me last night. Things that mean either she's crazy or there's more to Withernsea than I've been aware of."

Her eyes met mine. "You told him what we are?"

"I did. I hope that was okay?"

Shelley shrugged. "It's fine and we could have put him under a compulsion and wiped his mind anyway if we didn't want him to know."

"You could do what?" Henry spluttered. "It's real then? You're a witch and... other things."

Shelley spun blue threads from her hands and let her eyes turn blue, then she lifted up a vase from the hallway, got the door to bang open and threw it out so it exploded on the path.

Then she returned to normal. Looking all angelic like she'd not done anything strange at all. She shrugged her shoulders.

Theo rubbed at his head. "*What are you doing?*" His voice went higher and higher. "That's been in my family for generations."

Shelley went back to her blue-eyed state and using the blue webs commanded all the pieces back together and it appeared back in the hallway like it had never left.

"Oh yeah, I forgot you could do that. Sorry, darling."

Henry looked back at the doorway. "Oh yeah. I guess I should close it," Shelley said. "Could you do it, Theo?"

Theo whizzed there and back in a one-second blink of an eye. Henry looked back at the door. "How did you...?"

"Vampire speed."

"Oooh does Henry know what we are?" Mary came waltzing back in. "Did you miss me? Gosh I've been gaining tons of sexual experience. Such a pity that now Henry knows what I am a) I have someone and b) Henry's not dead which apparently makes us not compatible."

"You're too late anyway. Henry and Ebony are seeing each other, Mary," Shelley pointed out.

Mary smiled at me. "You lucky lady. I had a good look at him when he was changing into a fresh pair of overalls. I was almost invisible, so he never even knew I was there. Not everything about being dead sucks. Some things are positively delightful." She winked while pointing in the direction of Henry's groin.

"Mother! That's quite enough. When I get up later, we are going to be having a chat, you and I?"

"You'll have to catch me first, Son." Mary disappeared.

"Do you want to show me the computer programme so you can get to bed?" I asked Theo. He nodded.

What Theo had done was just beyond anything I could have hoped for. Customers could download a photo of themselves or input measurements and receive information on what stock I currently carried that should suit them the best.

"You should receive almost zero returns this way," he told me.

He'd also designed different 'model' templates of all different shapes and sizes where I could just drag the clothes across to demonstrate what they looked like, rather than me having to arrange photoshoots with lots of models. "Obviously you'll need to keep taking photos of your stock and uploading them, but from there the software will take over."

"That reminds me. Apparently, Henry is an amateur photographer. He could advise me about lighting so I can take the best photos of my stock."

"Did I hear my name?" Henry came walking in and looked at the website. "Okay, that's boring girly stuff, so what are you trying to get me to do because I don't look good in a skirt."

"I wondered if you'd show me how to take good photos and then I can upload good photographs of my stock."

"You want me and my camera in your shop, taking photos of clothes not on bodies? When?" His lip curled up at the edge.

"Tonight, maybe?"

"I'll see what I can do," he said. As he left the room again Theo turned to me.

"Get in there, Ebs," he said.

I nearly dropped through the floor in shock. The very strait-laced Theo was telling me to 'get in there'? What was happening to us both? We used to be cultured.

Love has happened and is happening.

Her voice came through to me loud and clear.

All is as it should be, Auntie Ebs. Enjoy and stay on the ride, even if the wheels start to come off.

A cold chill blew through me. What did Charlie mean?

On my way to my room later, Henry reached out and grabbed me. "Henry." I chastened him with my eyes. "While we're here we're working. I feel the same as you. I want to touch you all the time, but seriously, we need to concentrate."

"Err, I was just grabbing you because I wanted to tell you something."

"Oh," I said, disappointed despite my recent statement.

"You know how you told me you're here to protect the baby?"

"Ye-es."

"Well. I'm in. Whatever needs doing. If someone tries anything, I'll help anyway I can. I'm only a human, but a tin of paint bounced off someone's head can hurt a lot."

"You are one very special man, Mr Henry Marston." I lifted onto my tiptoes and kissed him softly on the lips. "It's a deal."

"Team Henebs, erm Ebshen, err. Oh fuck it," Henry said. "Team Ginger and Ebony."

"There's nothing finer than the combination of a rich dark chocolate and a sizzling ginger." I winked. "I'm talking biscuit combinations obviously."

"Obviously," he said, patting me on the backside as I turned away from him.

He'd called us a team.

He knew about my visions, and more than that he seemed to be believing what he was hearing now.

And he'd not run away.

I walked to my bedroom before he saw the happy tears spill from my eyes.

CHAPTER 16

EBONY

The last couple of weeks had passed without incident, and the supernaturals visiting Charlene had begun to peter out. Soon I would be able to move back home, which was fantastic as I'd be able to spend a lot more time with Henry. We'd been out every single night for the last fortnight, but I nearly always returned to my room at the farm. I just had a niggling feeling that something was going to happen. Things were going well between me and Henry though. I was quietly optimistic about the future.

Today's visitor was the leader of the Faeries of Withernsea. Mathilde was fair-haired, green-eyed, and arrived the size of a human, although it was known that when among their own, the faeries returned to their usual extremely small size and had gossamer wings.

She held Charlie in her hands and looked down at her in awe. "She is very beautiful."

The visit passed without incident. The gift of a small golden statue of a fairy was given to Charlie.

"We faeries welcome you into our kingdom, Charlene Landry."

I noted Mathilde didn't pledge her servitude or assistance, but that was the thing with faeries. They were wily creatures who liked to make deals. They weren't going to offer to help without seeing what they could get out of it.

Mathilde left and Shelley looked at me.

"It should be a crime to be that beautiful."

"Yes, but they're nowhere near as beautiful on the inside," I warned.

An hour later I was fixing lunch when my vision went dark. I saw Charlie's crib but the baby in it wasn't her.

My blood ran cold.

What the hell did I do?

The only thing I could do. I warned her mother.

Shelley went into a blind panic, asking me to repeat every detail of what I'd seen.

"That was it. I was given the image of the crib, but it wasn't Charlie in it. The baby was different." I sat with my head in my hands. "That's why I hate these visions. They give me part info that's not much use to anyone."

Shelley reached for my hand. "That's not true, Ebony. You've warned me of potential danger and now we shall be more ready than ever. Do you have any idea when it's going to take place?"

I shook my head sadly. "I don't know anything else. God, I feel useless."

Charlie. Do you know anything? Can you tell me?

Only that what's meant to be, will be. I'm sorry, Ebony. Fate makes the ultimate choices.

I remembered the vision she'd shown me days ago.

Recalling it gave me faith that everything would work out okay in the end.

Wards were strengthened.

Darius put police protection over the farmhouse.

Shelley moved the crib into her and Theo's room. We all said we'd take it in turns to look after Charlene.

All we could do was wait.

Two days later we found that when someone had a dastardly plan and was determined enough, they'd find a way.

Shelley had left Charlie in her crib in the living room while she went to answer the door. I got there at the same time as her. On opening it we found there was no one there.

"That's weird. Must be some kind of electrical fault," Shelley said, and she closed the door.

I followed her back into the living room and looked in the crib, to find it wasn't Charlene in there.

I screamed. Shelley followed my gaze and let out a heart wrenching guttural pain. "Noooooo. My baby."

Theo was downstairs in seconds. Panic ensued. The supernatural policeman was in the house just a minute later.

"How can it have happened? I only went to the door. There's been no forced entry. I just don't understand it. Who in their right mind abandons their baby and takes someone else's?"

And then it all clicked. "It's a faerie baby," I announced. "That's what it is. It's a changeling." I looked around the room. "Where's the gift they gave you? The statue?"

Shelley looked around frantically for it. "It's not here."

"It was a trick. The golden statue. It was a faerie. We had a faerie in the house all along. The wards wouldn't work because they were already here. I believe Mathilde has Charlene."

"Where does she live?" I took one look at Shelley's face and thanked the Lord I wasn't Mathilde de la Rey.

Shelley held onto me. "Sorry, Ebs, but I need you with me."

Then we travelled at a speed my body couldn't comprehend.

Outside Mathilde's large, detached house Shelley stood staring at the outside walls.

"Where do you think she'll be?" she asked Theo, then she turned to me. "Ebony, any idea?"

"I don't know, Shelley. She's not even necessarily at home." Then I thought about it. "Give me a second."

Charlie, can you hear me? We're outside Mathilde's. Are you there?

Yes. Second floor. She's standing with me at the window. I can see a large Oak tree. The woman is a crazy bitch. She keeps going on about how pretty I am and how she's going to add me to a collection. Bloody damn baby body. Help me, Ebs. Do not tell my mother you can talk to me. She'd not understand why it couldn't be her.

Okay, we're coming for you.

I did the only thing I could do. I faked a vision. I couldn't make my eyes roll in my head, so instead I acted like intense pain had hit my temples and I dropped face down on the grass.

"*Ebony*! Ebony, are you okay?"

"Second floor, Shelley. Looking out of the window at the Oak tree."

Shelley whizzed faster than I could see. The next thing I knew there was a blue light at the window of the house and then all the glass shattered outwards. A faerie flew out of the window dangling on a web. Mathilde reduced down to faerie size, but she couldn't escape Shelley's blue tendrils. If Shelley let it go, Mathilde would be able to fly away and escape. I ran as fast as my legs would carry me to just underneath the window.

"Shelley! Shelley!"

Shelley stood looking down at Mathilde, her face a mask of sheer hatred, fangs extended. Charlene was clutched in her arms surrounded by protective blue webs. The feral vampire was here.

"You dare take my child for your own, Mathilde de la Rey? Why should I not let my webs tear you to pieces and scatter your body parts across the land?"

"Help me. Help me please."

"Why?" Shelley yelled.

"I keep pretty things. Look at my house. It is full of them. Charlene is the prettiest thing I have ever seen. I couldn't resist."

I looked up at Shelley. "There's another way to hurt her. Think of it. Don't do something that takes you away from your daughter."

I saw when the penny dropped, and then so did Mathilde. She hit the grass on a soft landing as blue webs broke her fall. Mathilde's eyes were wide as she desperately tried to unfurl her gossamer wings. Shelley and Charlie appeared next to me. And then the sound of smashing and tinkling started.

Mathilde began to wail. "Please, no. Anything but that."

A blue sheet of what looked like a laser light passed through the whole house and I knew that it destroyed every single thing that Mathilde held dear.

"I shall be in touch with the faerie council immediately to have you removed from your position. Your punishment from me is concluded." Shelley eyes flashed red. "You come near my daughter again and I will gut you like a fish."

Mathilde ran away back towards her house.

I saw Shelley slump. Theo grabbed hold of her.

"Come on. Let's go home."

When we returned it was clear that Theo and Shelley just wanted to be alone with Charlene. Mary had sensed something wrong with her son and had rushed back. Security informed us that the changeling had been collected by two faeries while we were on our way home, and that they couldn't apologise enough, saying Mathilde would be dealt with in accordance with faerie policies.

"I'm going to go home and leave you guys to it. I'll be back in the morning."

Shelley passed Charlie to Theo and embraced me.

"Thank you. If it wasn't for you, we might never have got her back."

Me and Charlie, I thought. We made quite the team.

And now you are beginning to understand your role in all this a little more, my dear Aunt Ebs. Now go call Henry for a booty call. Let him strip more than just wallpaper.

It took a few days to get back to our normal. Shelley and Theo decided no more visitors were coming to the house and that instead they would hold a christening ceremony for Charlene. The supernaturals of Withernsea would be invited and anyone who still wished to pledge and hadn't yet, could do so there, where the spells would be iron cast and the security tighter than a Dita von Teese corset.

Henry had stayed at my house overnight and was on his way to a decorating job elsewhere. I was going to get the boutique ready for opening again and get some more stock on the website which I'd tentatively started.

"I was thinking." Henry grabbed his coat shrugging his arms into it. "Why don't we pop to the coffee shop tonight and tell Jax about us? Together. I reckon she'll be made up that I'm with you and horrified that you've chosen me."

"Don't be stupid. Yes, sounds good. After stocktaking, a coffee and a bun from your sister's coffee shop sounds just the thing. Wonder if I'll get an even bigger discount now I'm dating her brother?" I winked.

He gave me a lingering kiss in the doorway. "Do I really have to go to work?"

"Yes, you certainly do. My body needs a rest and I need to get to the shop."

"I love your body," he said. "I love every bit of it."

My heart palpitated loudly at him throwing the love word around, even though it was in terms of my body. I could feel a charge in the air.

"Well, you can love it some more tonight."

"I will," he said, looking at me just a beat too long. He turned and headed down the driveway and into his van.

CHAPTER 17

HENRY

I almost said it.

Fuck. I *wanted* to say it.

Those three little words.

But we'd only been together a few weeks.

And I'd accused *her* of being crazy.

All I knew was that in my whole two years with Callie it had *never* felt like this.

Maybe it was lust?

Maybe...

CHAPTER 18

EBONY

I t was difficult not to say anything when I called into Jax's for my usual early morning coffee.

"Ebony! I've missed seeing your face." She came over and flung her arms around me. "How have you been?"

"Good. Hopefully I'm back now and can get on with selling my clothes. How's business anyway?"

The coffee shop was busy with only one table spare. "Yeah, it's going well. I still haven't found anyone yet though. I think I'm being too picky. Perhaps instead of trying to entice customers I'm trying to do a Withernsea Dating and set myself up?"

I smiled. "Don't look too hard. I'm sure you'll meet someone in good time. Speaking of matchmaking. How are the terrible twosome doing?"

"Seriously. They're doing really well. Working dead hard. I've never seen either of them like this before, Ebs."

I sat back in my chair. "Something's going on with those two. I think I'll pay them a visit before I open up."

After finishing my drink, I made my way out of the

shop and up the back entrance of the dating agency. I still owned the building and I had a key so I let myself in.

"That client was mine. I opened the email first," Lucy was shouting.

"He's a supe. He's mine. You're covering humans," Kim yelled back.

"He's a centaur which makes him mostly an animal. Which of us covers animals because Shelley didn't specify?"

I walked into Kim's office where Lucy stood, hands on hips in front of Kim's desk. "Well, well. I hear you are both working extremely hard and indeed it's to the point where you are arguing for even more leads?"

They both looked at me guiltily.

"You might as well confess all because I've already seen it in a vision."

"You have? Does Shelley come back? Does she get rid of one of us? Or does she stay with Charlie and make me manager? Plus who gets the bonus payment?" Kim blabbed.

"Kim, you muppet. She's not had a vision. You are such a sucker... and a blabbermouth." Lucy looked at me. "Excuse me, Ebony. I have work to do." She left the room.

"Ebony! Did you not have a vision?"

"Nope. Just thought I'd get you to tell me what was going on."

"Damn it. I squealed like a pig."

"Let me get this straight. You're both working hard in case Shelley decides to stay home with Charlie, and to get a bonus?"

"Yes, because I should have the manager's position in

the bag, but Lucy is doing really well at bringing new clients in. You know how competitive we both are."

"Well, I've had a vision about Charlie which means I doubt you have to worry. I think Shelley will be back and all will return to as normal as it gets around here. I've no idea about the bonus though."

"She called me earlier. Told me about what went down with the faerie. It's really shaken her up."

"I know, but in a way it's been good because she handled it, and it also showed her that she's not invulnerable. There's always going to be a chance for the bad guys to misbehave. It's just about being as prepared as possible."

Kim nodded. "I think it's good she's having a christening for Charlie K. I don't know why she didn't do that in the first place instead of having to be polite to everyone separately. She can get this gig done in a day and go back to being a mum. Your vicar is performing the ceremony by the way. The one who you saw in a vision with his chorister. After a little bit of persuasion, they allowed Lucy to set them up. They've been dating ever since."

"Thank goodness that sometimes my visions do good, rather than cause chaos and confusion," I huffed.

"They brought me my husband. For which I am very, *very,* grateful. Although it did come after a lot of chaos and confusion."

"Only because you decided to date a rival shifter."

Kim stuck her tongue out at me. "Anyway, what about your piece of hot stuff? How's that going?"

I couldn't help it. A massive smile came over my face.

"Oh my god. Look at you. You're in love!"

I looked back at her shocked. "No, I'm not. It's going well, but it's far too early for love."

"Tell that to me and Darius when we eventually got together. To Shelley and Theo. To Frankie and Lucy. Things happen fast in Withernsea."

"Yes, well, I've always been the most sensible of all of you, so I think I'll take a little longer."

"If you say so." Kim gave me a look as if she didn't believe a word I was saying.

I wasn't sure I believed a word I was saying either.

At just after five Henry came into the shop.

"You're early."

"Yeah, I couldn't wait to see you." He came up to me behind the counter and wrapped me in a passionate embrace. "Come on. Let's get this visit to my sister over with, and then you can come to mine and see my etchings."

I giggled. "Okay then, let's go."

We walked into Jax's together hand in hand and watched as Jax's jaw hit her ankle boots. "You said you had a lovely new girlfriend. You didn't say it was one of my besties. Whooo hooo." She squealed and jumped up and down. Then she punched her brother in the arm. "You screw her over, Henry, and I'll kill you."

"Sorry, I already screwed her over... a chair, the bath-room sink..."

"Henry!" Jax and I shouted at the same time.

"Just no," I told him. "We invoke the best friend and

sister code. You cannot talk about sex while we are both here. Ever."

"Now tell me everything," Jax said. Then she paused. "You know what I mean. Everything about how you met."

We told her. We were like excited children.

Jax sat with her elbow resting on the table. Her chin was in her hand and her head tilted towards us. "Oh guys. I am so happy for you and so jealous. I need some love in my life."

"It's coming, Jax. Not yet awhile, but it's coming."

"It is?" She sat up. "Did you have a vision?"

"No. Ebony is just saying it's bound to happen sooner rather than later, right Ebs?"

Huh?

I turned to Henry. "No, that's not right," I said sternly. "Yes, I had a vision. But your hair was longer, Jax. In a bob, which shows it's not just yet."

"Oooh, and did you see who it is?"

"I did but his face was in shadow which means I'm not allowed to tell you."

"As long as I know he's coming. I was thinking about growing my hair. Now I definitely will. Thank you, Ebs." She looked at the counter. "Do you want any of the left-overs to take home either of you? I'll go bag some goodies up. I know Henry will want all the vanilla slices."

"Why did you do that?" Henry's voice had undertones of frustration and irritation.

"Do what?"

"Tell her you saw her with someone."

"Because I did."

"Yeah, but Jax doesn't know about the supernatural

shit, so why get her into predictions and stuff? You should just keep her out of all that."

I sat up very straight in my chair.

"Out of all the 'supernatural shit'. Is that how you see it, Henry? As total and utter 'shit'?"

"You're taking it all out of context. All I'm saying is she doesn't know about any of this. I'm trying to protect her."

"Protect her from what? Weirdos like me?"

"Don't be stupid. You're putting words in my mouth that I haven't said."

Jax came over. "What's going on? Is everything all right?"

"It's fine, Jax. We're just squabbling about him taking all the vanilla slices."

"Ah." Jax visibly relaxed. "Well, that's okay because I put one in your box anyway." She placed two cardboard cake boxes on the table. "Now I'd better get the place locked up. It was fantastic to see you both and I'm really happy for you. My brother and one of my besties." She smiled and re-hugged us both and then we left.

Henry moved closer and went to put an arm around me, but I shrugged him off. "I'm going to go back to my own house actually, Henry. I'm not in the mood tonight."

"Oh for fuck's sake. Just because I asked you to be careful around my sister."

"Your sister is going to end up with Tristan. You know, Tristan who you had the fight with? The pixie. You might want to let her get used to the world of the supernaturals because it's coming to Jax's life soon."

He backed away and folded his arms across his chest. "No way is he going anywhere near my sister."

"The visions said so."

"Well this time your visions are wrong."

"They're never wrong."

"This time they are. You'd better think up a new one, because that 'shit' isn't happening on my watch."

"I don't 'think visions up', you moron. They appear. She'll be happy with him, so don't you do anything to ruin it, you selfish bastard."

"She'll be happy? With that knob? If your brain saw Tristan as a good bloke, then you are definitely as cuckoo as I always thought."

I froze in place.

"Ebs, I didn't mean it like that."

I held my hand up. "Leave me alone, Henry. Just leave me the hell alone."

CHAPTER 19

SHELLEY

"I've called this emergency meeting because both Ebs and my brother are as miserable as sin, but they're both too stubborn to apologise," Jax said. "It's been a week now. I don't know what to do. Neither of them will say what caused it. They argued in here about vanilla slices, but it can't be that."

"I'll go and have a word with her," I reassured Jax. "Let me try to get to the bottom of it."

"Let me know if she's back on the market because Dmitri, the Hellhound footballer, hasn't found a match yet," Kim blurted.

"Desperate," Lucy snarked. "Totally and utterly desperate, Kim."

"The christening is in two days' time. If, when I've talked to Ebony, I think they both just need their heads banging together, then we try to get them to talk to each other there. Hopefully they'll come to their senses."

"How's everything at home now?" Jax asked me.

"Fine. Henry is back doing the decorating. We've

improved our security and we now have a scanner on entry that warns if anyone is trying to bring anything untoward into our home. We're okay now. We've got over the shock and we're being realistic. There are going to be other crises come up. I birthed the badass baby of Withernsea. We just have to relax the best we can and get on with things. So, I'll see you all at the christening. Now I'll go and find out what's happening with Ebony." I said my goodbyes and walked next door.

"Shelley! Where's the baby?" Ebony was packing clothes up at her counter and dropped them as I walked in.

"At home with Daddy. Theo was up by three today, so I thought I'd head over here and check on things. What's going on with you and Henry? And do not try to bullshit me."

Ebony sighed. "I saw Jax in a vision. She is going to fall in love with a supe. I told her, and Henry said I shouldn't be going on about my visions if she's to be kept out of the supe loop. When I told him who she's going to end up with—bearing in mind I confided in him as Jax can't know—he told me it was never going to happen. He's going to try to interfere with my visions which could cause who knows what trouble. I should never have trusted him."

"Who was it?"

She huffed. "Tristan."

I almost choked. "Jax... and Tristan?"

"Yes. I know it seems strange, but Jax is really tiny and her and Tristan will be the perfect fit."

"But he's an asshole!"

"With us. He won't be with her. She'll not put up with

it. I'm not saying they won't have their moments, but I saw them together and they looked happy."

"So at some point soon Jax will discover the truth about Withernsea?" I sighed. How was she going to feel when she found out we all knew and she didn't?

"Not if her brother has anything to do with it." Ebony raised her eyebrows.

"What are you doing here anyway? Are these online orders?" I picked up one of the dresses on her counter. That actually brought a smile to my friend's face. "Yes! It's working amazingly. I can't thank Theo enough. One of these is going to all the way to France."

"Ebony, that's fabulous."

"I've not had many visions in the last week or so. It's been nice to have something to keep me busy."

"You're missing Henry, aren't you?"

"Yes." Ebony chewed on her bottom lip, and she blinked her eyes a few times. "But he said I was as cuckoo as he first thought. I think I can safely say we're through."

"Oh, Ebony." I gave her a hug. I was going to be having words with Mr Marston when he came to paint tomorrow.

"Are you ready for your very important role of Charlene's godmother?"

"I am. I'm honoured. Hopefully Kim will let me get a look in with the baby."

"Who knows what Kim's going to be like? I don't think Fate herself can predict her behaviour. If she gets out of control, I promise to bind her in my webs. That's all I can do."

"Thanks for dropping by, Shelley." Her gaze dropped to the floor.

"Hey, look at me."

She did, but she sighed.

"You have been there for me all through my meeting Theo, and through Charlie's birth. It's time I was there for you. I'm here, Ebs. Whenever you need me."

"You were. You were there for me when my visions disappeared. That's what friends are for. Thanks, Shelley. It's appreciated, but I'll be okay. If my visions are to be believed, my husband is still out there somewhere." She clicked onto the screen in front of her.

"Oh my god!"

"What?"

She pointed to the screen and to a web page that said 'new arrivals'. "This is one of the places I get my stock from. She's showing the next season's styles. These will be available to buy from August this year."

"Oh, you were just getting excited about new stock. I thought it was something important." My own idea of clothes shopping was a couple of pairs of jeans about every five years, then waiting until they basically fell apart before I had to buy anything else, so unfortunately I didn't share Ebony's enthusiasm.

"It is important. Shelley, look at this dress."

On screen she clicked through to a beautiful pale blue dress with capped sleeves, and a short 'v' neck. It came to just below the knee and was covered in the most delicate lace. It was vintage style and absolutely beautiful.

"I have to say that is lovely. I think you'll sell a lot of those."

"It's not for the shop, Shelley. They are the bridesmaid

dresses in my vision. Which means my wedding can't be that far away."

Henry had left by the time I returned, but he was back by the next morning. As he walked through the door, I wrapped a tendril of blue web around him that picked him up and dragged him into the living room where I sat cuddling my daughter.

"What the hell is happening? Arrrgh."

I dropped him in the chair opposite and then I bound his feet together and secured his waist to the chair.

Mary appeared. "Sorry, Shelley. I heard a commotion and thought I'd better check no one was trying to abduct my granddaughter. I didn't realise you and Theo had an open relationship and that you were into kink. Guess it's weird if the mother-in-law joins in with this part, right?"

"Ewwww, Mary. I've captured Henry because he has pissed my friend off and he isn't leaving here until I get some answers."

"Oh," Mary said. "I'll go back to what I was doing then, which was Alistair, by the way."

"Mary!"

"I'm going. I'm going. Sorry I can't show off because I have a boyfriend for the first time in a century."

With Mary gone, I turned back to my captive.

"What is this I hear about you calling my friend cuck-oo?" I narrowed my eyes at him. "And just remember you are answering a witch, vampire, and wyvern cross who currently rules the whole of Withernsea so you might want to be honest. Because I haven't shown you even a thousandth of my powers." I let my fangs descend and my eyes go red.

"I was a dick, all right? She was telling my sister about her visions, and she doesn't know but Jax has had a really bad time with her lack of a love life. There have been occasions when I've had to drag her out of the flat because she's been low, convinced she'll never meet anyone. I didn't want Ebony giving her false hope. It would be cruel." He scrubbed a hand through his beard. "And then she said it was bloody Tristan."

"Yes, I have to admit I probably had a similar reaction to yours when she told me that."

"After all she's been through, I don't want my sister to end up with an arsehole."

I let out a deep exhale.

"Look, Henry. I can tell you that what Ebony sees is either a warning or a prediction of love and she says Jax and Tristan will be together. Will love each other. No one could have told me that I'd end up married to a vampire. I was a human who had no idea of the supernaturals living here, just like you were and just like Jax is. It's her future and she'll work things out and get there. I can't tell you it will be plain sailing because Ebony saw Kim's happy ever after, but then she also saw a potential pack war. Kim was held hostage before she and Darius were able to get together."

"Is this supposed to help me?"

"I'm just saying that none of this is straightforward. But is life easy anyway? Even without the supernatural element. Look at you and Callie. You had problems and she cheated on you. You don't need a paranormal element for things to go awry."

"I suppose not."

"Now, it's like this, Henry. It's Charlie's christening on Saturday. If you still want Ebony as your girlfriend, then you'd better sort things out either before or while you're there and before the ceremony starts. I don't want to hear you arguing on what is a special day for my family. If you aren't interested in carrying things on with her, then break it to her gently, but after the party, you hear?"

"Loud and clear. Okay, I will sort things out. I really l-like her you know."

I sat stunned. "You paused, Henry. You said l-like."

"I've got a bit of a stammer."

"Witch, wyvern, vampire."

"Okay, I think I might be starting to love her, all right?" Henry blushed which looked endearing on him.

I beamed.

"And for that I won't render you permanently impotent." I removed all the webs. "You can get on with the painting now. I have to say, it's coming along really well. Can I talk to you at some point about decorating this room?"

"Err, yes. Of course. Maybe next week?" Henry backed out of the room and for a moment I honestly thought he might pee himself. Sometimes I think I had a little too much fun with my powers.

I looked at my daughter. "That's him told, isn't it, babes?"

I got a little windy smile in return and a gurgle so I guessed she agreed.

Chapter 20

Ebony

It was Charlie's christening day. March's many weathers had decided to give us a bright sunny day with no rain, although I did wonder if Shelley had pulled in a favour from Mother Nature, who apparently was the best friend of Angel Sophia. It had meant that I'd been able to dress in a mint-green shift dress with a fitted jacket over the top. A small hat with lace on it completed my look. My hair was in a smart chignon. I'd become obsessed with Meghan Markle since her engagement to Prince Harry had been announced, and I was stalking her looks online. I couldn't help but compare me and Henry with them. Unfortunately, me and Henry were no dream couple; more like a nightmare.

I arrived at the Church early, and as people arrived, I greeted familiar faces including the other godmother, Kim; and Darius, who had been chosen as godfather.

"There are some beautiful outfits here today, Ebs. About what percentage of them are you responsible for?"

I smiled. "About 90% and I made sure no one bought the same thing."

"Business is booming then?" Darius asked.

"Absolutely. In the last couple of days I've not had time to stand still with people coming in last minute for christening outfits. The web page orders have increased too."

"And not a drop of vodka in sight?" Kim queried.

"Not one. All I get now is a kind of buzzing in my head, like a warning. It gives me time to sit down somewhere, so people aren't getting to see my eyes roll either which is a bonus."

"I guess in some ways that evil warlock did you a favour, because after, your visions have changed in how they present to you."

"Absolutely." It wasn't the truth, but I had no other way to explain the situation without giving Charlie away or sounding like I really was cuckoo.

I looked around at the milling guests and there he was talking to Rav—Henry. He spotted me looking at him, so I turned my head away from him quickly.

But he just couldn't leave it there. The next minute he was standing at the side of me.

"Can I have a word?"

"You can have two, and together they make a sentence that before I was too much of a lady to utter. However, for you I think I'll make an exception."

"Please, Ebony. I'm sorry. Let me apologize."

Shelley and Theo chose that moment to walk up to us. Shelley spoke. "The ceremony is about to start. The vicar wants to chat to us about our roles in Charlene's life. Henry, would you hold Charlie while we talk to him?"

"But what if one of these weirdos tries something? I'm human. I don't have any superpowers to protect her."

"Mary's going to keep an eye on you. Her and Alistair are around. They just can't be seen. She'll let me know if anything strange occurs. Plus, there's so much protective magic here. It's only for a moment. You'll be fine. If I didn't think so, I wouldn't ask."

"Okay then." He took Charlie from Shelley, and I had to swallow past the lump in my throat at seeing this hunky man standing holding a cute baby.

Ovaries, pipe down.

We walked inside and met Alexander the vicar. As he spoke, he was eloquent, and you could see the kindness radiating from him. The choir were getting together in the background, and I knew which man was his new boyfriend because the guy couldn't take his eyes off him. He talked to us briefly about what the role of godparent was about. Alex said he preferred to do it that way and to keep the ceremony itself brief and to the point because he knew people got bored in church fast.

We walked back out of the church to let people know it was almost time for the ceremony to start. But before we could utter a word, we all stood like someone had yelled 'freeze' in a game of musical statues as Henry came around the corner of the church with a tall brunette. She was dressed in a white silk dress with a lacy overcoat which I knew I had in my collection at the boutique.

"Where the hell is my daughter?" Shelley screamed. "How dare he abandon her for some tart, and I can't even kill him because there are other humans here."

Mary appeared at the side of us.

"Oh, Shelley. I really didn't see this coming. Look at her."

"I am looking at her. Oh, for heaven's sake. How young is she? She only looks like a teenager. What's he playing at? I warned him what I'd do if he hurt my friend."

She did?

As the woman got closer, I realised exactly who Henry was with.

Charlene.

In the vision she'd shown me she'd been in her early twenties, but right now, baby Charlene was a teen.

"Where's my baby?" Shelley screamed at him. I put a hand up to him and pulled Shelley and Theo to one side. I whispered to them. "Look closer at Henry's companion. Look at the curve of her rosebud lips and the blue of her eyes. At the dark brown of her hair like her dad's. It is your daughter. It's Charlene."

Shelley caught hold of her daughter's arm and peered closely at her.

"How the hell?"

"Hey, Mum, Dad. *Surprise!*" Charlie grinned.

Theo stood stock still and then he passed clean out, hitting the floor.

"Auntie Kim, Uncle Darius, can you get everyone into the church? Explain to the vicar that there's a slight delay, and Henry, can you help me carry my dad to a bench?"

Within a few minutes we were alone outside, just me, Henry, Charlie, Shelley, and Theo.

Theo sat with his head in his hands as he came around. Shelley turned to her daughter. "Please explain this to me because I've seen a lot over the past year, but I'm sure I just had a baby a few weeks ago and now I appear to have a teenage daughter."

Theo groaned.

"Basically, Mum, I had an older brain even though I was in a baby body, so the last few weeks have been kinda rough. You know the whole 'not in control of my bowels stuff'? I can't rule Withernsea in a baby body and I'm supernatural including being part vampire. By the time I'm a year old I'll be in a twenty-year-old's body. This right now is another interim stage. I need a little while to gather some more energy."

"But I'm here in the meantime. Why have you had to grow so fast? I was enjoying cuddling my little baby. Now you're taller than I am!"

"The war is coming, Mum. Soon you will hear the first rumble of it. Plus, I really don't get why you were expecting me to grow and act like a human baby when there's only a bit of human from Grandad Dylan in the mix. Not only do I have my genetic traits, but I can take on any of the supernatural traits of those I rule over. I'm just so lit!"

Shelley huffed out, making her top lip vibrate. "My pregnancy was accelerated so I shouldn't be all that surprised that your aging is. You're not going to get old and die quickly, are you?" The panic in Shelley's expression was evident.

"No, Mum. I'm just going to settle around my early twenties for a while. But how about right now, let's just spend some time with me as a teenager? It's going to be for a year or so. Henry, you're going to need to decorate my room again because the whole teddy bears thing really isn't doing it for me. That reminds me, I need to buy some Sean Mendes posters."

"His music videos made you really settled."

"I was just staring at the man candy, Mum. Although yeah, his tunes rock too."

Theo looked at Charlie and then back at Shelley. "Let me get this straight. My daughter is now a pretty teenager who has way more powers than I do, and she likes boys?"

"You got it, Pops."

Theo stood up to his full height and walked right up to his daughter. "I'm still going to ground you if you step out of line, and no boyfriends unless I've vetted them through my entire database first." He paused. "Did I just say boyfriends when an hour ago I just changed my daughter's nappy?"

He looked very queasy again, but he got hold of his daughter and embraced her in a massive hug. "I love you, Charlene Landry."

"Love you too, Dad."

"Is everything okay?"

Kai the merman walked out of church dressed once again in his sparkly, scale-patterned tight trousers. He took one look at Charlie and blanched and then blushed.

"Is this you, Charlene?"

How did he know?

"You got it, Kai. But you're still a little old for me yet so hang in there okay, baby? I'll call you. Be about a year? Feel free to go get some more experience in the meantime."

"CHARLENE KIMBERLY LANDRY," Theo exploded. His fangs bared, he stood hissing in Kai's direction before composing himself. "Kai, get back into church and away from my daughter or my fangs are going to act like a fishing line on you. You. Get. ME?"

Kai dropped to a bow. "No trouble intended, Mr Landry. I just came outside because people are becoming agitated wondering what's happening."

"What's happening is I'm getting christened. Let's go," Charlie said.

On our way into church, she grabbed hold of my arm. "Auntie Ebs, couple of things. One, I had to whizz over to the shop and find myself an outfit, so my dad owes you for this dress. Two, it's okay, I did compulsion on Henry so he doesn't remember that in front of his eyes I shimmered and then he had a naked sixteen-year-old in his arms. He wouldn't have got over that. Would have taken a LOT of therapy, so I blanked him."

"I'm not interested in the subject of Henry Marston. Your outfit is a present. You can come to my shop any time. I guess you're going to need a whole new wardrobe."

"Yeeaasss. I was hoping you were going to say that. It's fabulous having an auntie who owns a boutique."

"You know I'm not your auntie, right?"

She looked over her shoulder to where Debbie and Mark Linley were sitting with Polly. "Those two. They want to be part of the family but it's too much for them. They want me to call them my grandparents, but I won't. Some people aren't deserving of it. YOU are deserving of the name auntie whether you are related to me by blood or not, and of course my Auntie Kim's going to just try to lead me all kinds of astray so you need to balance that out."

Shelley and Theo had a quick word with the vicar which included compulsion so that he was led to believe the christening was to baptise a teenager after all. I had to admit it was a handy skill. If I wasn't a supe, I'd ask them to wipe out the fact I missed Henry.

"Not a chance, Auntie Ebs. You're meant to be."

"You're reading my mind? That's still a thing?"

"You betcha. We need our mind link to stay intact for the future."

"Is what's coming bad, Charlie?"

"I don't know. All I know is there will be a war and I have a huge responsibility. I have to read all the prophecy stuff and figure it out."

"You'll need to talk to Frankie."

"There's plenty of time for that. Let's get this boring thing done now so we can go party."

———

The ceremony passed without a hitch and a lot of the supernatural community went home afterwards. However, Jax had set up a small buffet back at the coffee shop for those who wanted to go back.

"Mmmmm, Jax. I have wanted one of these doughnuts for ages. They are to die for."

Jax looked at Charlie strangely. "Er, great." She looked over at Theo and Shelley, then back at me. "Where's the baby?"

"Jax, what colour do you think my eyes are?" Charlie asked her and I watched as she used compulsion on Jax so she believed she'd always been around. We needed to let Jax in on the secrets of Withernsea. This wasn't fair playing with our friend's mind like that. Compulsion or not, she was going to work out that some things just didn't add up.

Darius' sister Alyssa ran over to Charlie, and Jax moved away, back to making sure everyone had food and drink.

"Hey, Charlie. I'm Darius' sister Alyssa. We're almost the same age. Wanna hang?"

"God, yeah, totally. I totes agree we should be besties like you said when you visited. You can tell me where we can go that's not dullsville. Do you like Sean Mendes?"

"He is hawt. Oh and we can totally put our powers together and play pranks on people." Alyssa winked.

"Well, duh."

Darius turned to Theo. "I think we need an alcoholic beverage, my friend."

My head buzzed with the inkling of a coming vision, and so I excused myself and walked just outside the doorway. I let it take over me and then I sniggered. Hell yes!

My vision returned, and I found Henry standing in front of me.

My smile fell off my face. "Not you again."

"Ebony. I was a shit to you. I know this. Please forgive me for what I said. It's true when I first met you, I did think you were cuckoo. I'm a human, Ebs, and your eyes, they really do look all kinds of weird when they roll and I can only see the whites. But now I've realised that everyone in Withernsea is bloody cuckoo. Including me. I'm cuckoo for you, Ebs. I just can't cope without you in my life. I know it's early days, but I love you, Ebony. Please don't let this end."

I shook my head as if dislodging a water blockage from my ear like you get from the shower sometimes. "Pardon?"

He grabbed my hands in his. "I love you. We've been dating for only a few weeks, but I know what my heart feels,

Ebs. I need you in my arms, and in my bed every night." He dropped to one knee.

"I'm aware this is crazy, and we can have a long engagement, but I don't want anyone else, and no way are you dating anyone else because I'd die. Ebony Yolanda Walker, will you marry me?"

Stunned didn't come close. I heard Charlie's voice in my head. *Look inside your heart, Ebs. What's there? That's your answer.*

I did, and there I saw love.

"Yes," I told him, nodding my head and giggling. "Yes. I love you too and I will marry you, but not right now. We need to get to know each other better."

"Oh, I intend to get to know every inch of you, Ebony." And then my vision went dark again.

It's against the rules to show you your own future, Auntie Ebs, but hey I'm gonna rule the place so they can kiss my arse. Just a sneak peek. mind you...

I saw myself at the entrance of the church and as I spun around there he was, hurtling through the door. "Ebony, I'm sorry I'm late."

The vision changed, and we were at the front of the church and Alexander pronounced us man and wife.

The vision ended, and my sight returned.

Not a word to anyone else, Auntie Ebs. And I'm totally chief bridesmaid or else.

You got it, Charlie. Thank you.

After making sure I was okay, Henry picked me up, spun me around and then let me slide back down him until my feet touched the floor. His lips met mine and fireworks sizzled throughout my body.

And my future was sealed.

CHAPTER 21

CHARLIE

Seriously, these two had looked like they were going to faff about for years. None of us had time for that. I'd just used a teeny tiny bit of acceleration on their emotions to bring on the instalove. None of us needed to endure a couple of years of them bickering and then getting back together, even if angry hate sex was probably kind of fun. I let them realise what they would have done eventually. That they totally loved each other.

My eyes looked around the room.

At my mum and dad who were smiling and gazing into each other's eyes. At Frankie and Lucy who were hung onto each other's every word. At Uncle Darius and Auntie Kim who kept pinching each other's bottoms. There was so much love in the room. My eyes caught those of Mark and Debbie. They smiled at me tentatively. It wasn't the look you gave a grandchild you loved dearly. Instead, they stared at me like I was an unexploded bomb.

When really... they were.

Polly gazed around the room until her eyes landed on Drake's.

It had started.

Ebony walked in hand-in-hand with Henry.

"We're getting married," she squealed. She whispered to me, "Sorry for stealing your christening thunder."

"Ah, I'm getting out of here anyway. Me and Alyssa are going to watch Sean Mendes videos and talk boys."

"Don't let your father hear you say that." She took my arm. "Look, take it easy with him. Maybe go back to the house now rather than go out with your friend. Let him get used to the fact he has a teenage daughter."

"But I'm scared if I go home he's gonna have me locked up in magic. He's going to make me a Rapunzel. I know it!"

"Your father loves you dearly. You might be the future badass ruler of Withernsea, but he will always want to protect you. Let him think he can, even though we know you're stronger than all of us. It's what dad's do."

"You're right. I'll go tell Alyssa that I need to spend time with the parentals."

"Charlie." Kim came dashing over. "Time for me to start being a naughty auntie. Try this gin drink. It's pink and lovely."

Ebony took it out of Kim's hand. "Don't be ridiculous. Do you want Theo fainting again?" She placed it on the table behind me.

"Give it back then," she protested.

"I'm afraid I can't. You see you can't be drinking it

either." Ebony smiled. A slow spreading smile that she then accompanied with a raise of her brows until I watched the penny drop.

Kim's chin hit the floor.

"What did you just say?"

"There's more than one. That's all I'm allowed to tell you." Ebony guffawed with laughter.

"*What?* More than one? Like two, three, fuck, am I having like six? What about my figure? Do I give birth as a wolf or as a human? Please tell me they won't wreck my vagina. Oh my god, Dar-iii-uuusss." She went running back to him.

"You enjoyed that far too much, Auntie Ebony."

She held up a high-five. I slapped it back.

"Go be with your man," I said.

"I hope you get time to just be a teen, Charlie. To enjoy yourself and have fun. That it's not all Withernsea woes."

I shrugged my shoulders.

"What will be will be," I said, and I walked away.

CHAPTER 22

EBONY

September 2018

Withernsea had managed a whole six months without too much supernatural mayhem. Most of the hi-jinx had come from the very spirited duo of Charlie and Alyssa.

Shelley had returned to work at the dating agency, and Charlie had come to work with me in the boutique, helping me run the online side which had grown beyond anything one person could handle. When Shelley had gone back to work, Lucy had suggested to Frankie that they go on a research trip around the world looking into the history of supernaturals. They'd only got back last week. Henry and I had sat down and spoken to Jax about the supernaturals of Withernsea. After a few hours of hysteria, and a large bottle of wine later, she had slowly started to come around to the idea. She was now at the stage where things were making a lot more sense. Like how Shelley would have had to have been around ten to have Charlie. Before Jax's brain would just get stuck when she tried to make sense of it. Now everything was becoming clear. As Jax could be known for being very sensitive, when she'd started to get a little upset that she'd been the only one kept out of the loop, I told her my visions had shown me it had to be that way in readiness for her future love. It was a little white lie, but it stopped her from closing the coffee shop in a huff and denying us the drink of the gods.

Theo spent much of his time monitoring his daughter's social media accounts. After much soul searching, he'd put a halt on his Bed and Breakfast plans saying having a teenage daughter was enough for him to deal with right now. Plus, now his mother wasn't around much, he and Shelley got to spend a lot more time together when Charlie was out, and he was making the most of it. Like he said, he had years to open and run a B&B. I guess to a 127-year-old vampire, a delay of a year or two was nothing.

"The car is here, Ebony. Are you ready?"

I didn't have a father, but my grandmother had come to walk me down the aisle and give me away. I was helped into the wedding car and then we were on our way.

"Your mother would have been proud of you," my Grandma said. I knew she was right. My mum would have been happy that I'd found love. I touched the diamond bracelet on my wrist that had belonged to her. My something old. *Thank you, Mama.*

My something blue was of course the bridesmaid dresses. The bridesmaids were waiting for me outside the church when I arrived. Shelley and Charlie waved as I pulled up in the car whereas Kim was yelling at Darius.

I got out and went up to them.

Kim looked at me. "You look absolutely stunning, you cow." She looked down at her enormous baby bump. "At no point when you had your wedding visions did you notice I was heavily pregnant. Really? How'd you miss this?"

"I told you. I only saw your chest upwards."

"Huh. I could have used a heads up that not only would I be having triplets, but that this overprotective, overbearing idiot would be in my personal space. Go inside, Darius, before I bite your throat out."

"Darius, unless you want me to dress you in a lovely blue dress too, I suggest you take your seat."

He growled. "Fine. But as soon as the ceremony is over, I will be right back at your side protecting my cubs, wife."

"Christ, you're doing my head in. Shelley, Charlie, can't you put a spell on him or something?"

Darius finally went into the church. "We can't go in there yet. The groom hasn't arrived," Shelley said.

"He'll be here, don't worry," I told her, and I met Charlie's gaze and smiled.

My dress was white, form fitting and plain. I'd totally gone a little Duchess of Sussex except my dress had a sweetheart neckline.

I took a deep breath and waited.

The sound of a car hurtling up the driveway came, the noise of stones thrown out in its wake accompanying it. Henry dashed through the door a few moments later. "Ebony, I'm sorry I'm late. Bloody wedding car wouldn't start and none of us had a mobile phone between us to let you know."

"I wasn't worried. I knew you'd be here. Shall we?" I asked him.

Then we walked down the aisle together.

And just like in my vision the vicar pronounced us husband and wife.

We'd hired the village hall for our reception. It seemed a very long time ago that I'd visited there during a speed dating event in order to tell Theo that his wife was on her way. Now he had a wife and a daughter.

And now I had a husband!

A very sexy husband who was giving me 'I can't wait to get out of here and get you into bed' eyes.

The DJ announced it was time for our first dance and I grasped his hand. Henry led me to the dance floor.

As we danced to *Beautiful Day* by *U2*, we invited everyone onto the dance floor with us. People made their way forwards, and I saw Tristan look around before his eyes settled on Jax. He walked over and asked her to dance.

"So, Mrs Marston, have you had any visions today? Such as ones where we go to bed and don't get out for a week?"

I shushed him. "We can't go anywhere yet. We have all these guests still here."

He groaned. "The bridesmaid's dresses aren't the only things blue around here." He pointed to his pants.

"Henry, behave yourself."

"Spoilsport."

Then Shelley's parents gate-crashed the reception. Stomping across the dance floor, they interrupted Shelley who had been wrapped in her husband's arms.

"Shelley," Debbie yelled.

"Huh? What are you doing here? Is everything all right?"

"No, it most certainly is not all right," Debbie huffed. "I just found my daughter in bed with one of your supernatural creatures."

"Ooh, which one?" Kim asked, walking nearer before Darius pulled her back.

"Well, she was yelling the name Drake out loud," Mark said.

"Lord Drake? Good for her," Kim said, making a loud growl escape from Darius' mouth.

"You do know Polly can make her own mind up about who she dates, right?" Shelley told them, folding her arms across her chest.

Charlie moved onto the dance floor and gave a nod in my direction.

I'll sort out these selfish idiots.

Holding my new husband's hand, I began to lead him off the dance floor.

"Where are we going?"

"Home."

"I thought you said...?"

"It has just been pointed out to me that when you have something enormous on your mind that you don't take other peoples' feelings into consideration. You just press on regardless."

"They were very rude, turning up like that. You should have let me throw them out."

"Yes, well like I say, they reminded me that I have something enormous on *my* mind, so let's get out of here."

"I don't need telling twice, wife." Henry picked me up and carried me out of the room.

I smiled. Right now, my vision was full of a hot husband who was eager to have his wicked way with me, and that suited me just fine.

No matter what was around the corner, we would face it together. Because Henry had been destined for me. Here for the seer.

THE END

Can Polly and Drake get together, or will it spell war in Withernsea?

Find out in the fifth book in the series, *Didn't Sea it Coming.*

For a glimpse of life before the vampire got his wife, join my mailing list and receive the short story prequel *Dating Sucks*:

geni.us/andiemlongparanormal

About Andie

Andie M. Long lives in Sheffield, UK, with her long-suffering partner, her son, and a gorgeous Whippet furbaby. She's addicted to coffee and Toblerone.

When not being partner, mother, or writer, she can usually be found wasting far too much time watching TikTok.

Andie's Reader Group on Facebook
www.facebook.com/groups/haloandhornshangout

TikTok and Instagram
@andieandangelbooks

Paranormal Romance
BY ANDIE M. LONG

Supernatural Dating Agency

The Vampire wants a Wife

A Devil of a Date

Hate, Date, or Mate

Here for the Seer

Didn't Sea it Coming

Phwoar and Peace

Also on audio, paperback, and a complete series ebook bundle available.

The Paranormals

Hex Factor

Heavy Souls

We Wolf Rock You

Satyrday Night Fever

Also in paperback. Complete series ebook available.

Sucking Dead

Suck My Life – available on audio.

My Vampire Boyfriend Sucks

Sucking Hell

Suck it Up

Hot as Suck

Filthy Rich Vampires – Reverse Harem

Royal Rebellion (Last Rites/First Rules duet) – Time Travel
Young Adult Fantasy

Immortal Bite – Gothic romance

Printed in Great Britain
by Amazon